The Journey Prize Stories

Winners of the $10,000 Journey Prize

1989
Holley Rubinsky for "Rapid Transits"

1990
Cynthia Flood for "My Father Took a Cake to France"

1991
Yann Martel for "The Facts Behind the Helsinki Roccamatios"

1992
Rozena Maart for "No Rosa, No District Six"

1993
Gayla Reid for "Sister Doyle's Men"

1994
Melissa Hardy for "Long Man the River"

1995
Kathryn Woodward for "Of Marranos and Gilded Angels"

1996
Elyse Gasco for "Can You Wave Bye Bye, Baby?"

1997 (shared)
Gabriella Goliger for "Maladies of the Inner Ear"
Anne Simpson for "Dreaming Snow"

1998
John Brooke for "The Finer Points of Apples"

1999
Alissa York for "The Back of the Bear's Mouth"

2000
Timothy Taylor for "Doves of Townsend"

2001
Kevin Armstrong for "The Cane Field"

2002
Jocelyn Brown for "Miss Canada"

The Journey Prize Stories

From the Best of
Canada's New Writers

Selected by Michelle Berry,
Timothy Taylor, and Michael Winter

National Library of Canada Cataloguing in Publication

The Journey Prize stories.

"From the best of Canada's new writers".
Annual.
15-
Continues: The Journey Prize anthology.
ISSN 1707-9640
ISBN 0-7710-4410-0 (volume 15)

1. Short stories, Canadian (English).
2. Canadian fiction (English) – 21st century.

PS8329.J68   C813'.010806   C2003-904912-4

We acknowledge the financial support of the Government of Canada through the Book Publishing Industry Development Program and that of the Government of Ontario through the Ontario Media Development Corporation's Ontario Book Initiative. We further acknowledge the support of the Canada Council for the Arts and the Ontario Arts Council for our publishing program.

"Reaching" © Rosaria Campbell; "The Lemon Stories" © Hilary Dean; "Hansel and Gretel" © Dawn Rae Downton; "Gay Dwarves of America" © Anne Fleming; "Truth" © Elyse Friedman; "Hush" © Charlotte Gill; "My Husband's Jump" © Jessica Grant; "Conversion Classes" © Jacqueline Honnet; "Resurrection" © S.K. Johannesen; "Cuckoo" © Avner Mandelman; "Night Finds Us" © Tim Mitchell; "The Difference Between Me and Goldstein" © Heather O'Neill.
These stories are reprinted with permission of the authors.

The quote on page 154 is from *Hop on Pop* by Dr. Seuss, published by Random House Books for Young Readers.

Typeset in Trump Mediaeval by M&S, Toronto
Printed and bound in Canada

McClelland & Stewart Ltd.
The Canadian Publishers
481 University Avenue
Toronto, Ontario
M5G 2E9
www.mcclelland.com

1 2 3 4 5   07 06 05 04 03

About *The Journey Prize Stories*

The $10,000 Journey Prize is awarded annually to a new and developing writer of distinction. This award, now in its fifteenth year, and given for the third time in association with the Writers' Trust of Canada as the Writers' Trust of Canada/ McClelland & Stewart Journey Prize, is made possible by James A. Michener's generous donation of his Canadian royalty earnings from his novel *Journey*, published by McClelland & Stewart in 1988. The winner of this year's Journey Prize will be selected from among the twelve stories in this book.

The Journey Prize Stories comprises a selection from submissions made by literary journals across Canada, and, in recognition of the vital role journals play in discovering new writers, McClelland & Stewart makes its own award of $2,000 to the journal that has submitted the winning entry. This year the selection jury comprises three acclaimed authors: Michelle Berry is the author of two critically acclaimed short-story collections, *How to Get There from Here* and *Margaret Lives in the Basement*, and the novels *What We All Want* and *Blur*. She is also the author of a collaborative art/fiction book entitled *Postcard Fictions* and the co-editor (with Natalee Caple) of *The Notebooks: Interviews and New Fiction from Contemporary Writers*. She lives in Toronto. Timothy Taylor is the author of the novel *Stanley Park*, a finalist for The Giller Prize, and the fiction collection *Silent Cruise*. He won the 2000 Journey Prize, and is the only writer ever to have three stories published in a single edition of the *Journey Prize* anthology. His short fiction has appeared in Canada's leading literary magazines and has been anthologized widely. He lives in Vancouver. Michael Winter is the author of two short-story collections, *One Last Good Look* and *Creaking in Their Skins*, and the novel *This All Happened*, winner of the Winterset Award and a finalist for the Rogers Writers' Trust Fiction Prize. He divides his time between St. John's and Toronto.

The Journey Prize Stories (formerly known as *The Journey Prize Anthology*) has established itself as one of the most prestigious anthologies in the country. It has become a who's who of up-and-coming writers, and many of the authors whose early work has appeared in the anthology's pages have gone on to single themselves out with collections of short stories and literary awards. The Journey Prize itself is the most significant monetary award given in Canada to a writer at the beginning of his or her career for a short story or excerpt from a fiction work in progress.

McClelland & Stewart would like to acknowledge the continuing enthusiastic support of writers, literary journal editors, and the public in the common celebration of the emergence of new voices in Canadian fiction.

For more information about *The Journey Prize Stories*, please consult our Web site: www.mcclelland.com/jps

Contents

Congratulations to the Journey Prize
– from the Authors

"Being nominated for the Journey Prize made me feel as if my choice to be a writer was not entirely wayward. Of course, I had friends who encouraged me, friends who also wrote (better than I did, some of them), but . . . there is nothing like the approval of strangers to make you feel you're on the right track. Not that the nomination was more important than the opinion of my friends, the (obsessive) reading I did, the music I listened to, the sheer, ceaseless thinking about writing, but . . . it simply made me feel I had (at least once) managed to make my private universe available to those with no vested interest in me whatsoever. That, a kind of recognition across a divide, gave me a confidence in the road I had chosen. I might still be mistaken for devoting my life to writing. There is still time for all to end badly, but . . . if there is some ledger, some means of tabulating the positive (on one side) and the negative (on the other), the Journey Prize nomination is (almost certainly) on the good side of things. . . . In any case, I am still writing, and I am grateful to James Michener, to McClelland & Stewart, to the jury that gave me a (sadly brief) confidence in my work."   – André Alexis

"For storytellers and those brave souls who publish them, the *Journey Prize* anthology is a celebration and barometer of new Canadian writing. Inclusion is its own reward and recognition, and the Prize itself a windfall shared by some very fine company. I was on an island six thousand kilometres away when I received word. There could be no finer homecoming."

– Kevin Armstrong

"I've been thinking about the *Journey Prize* anthology and, aside from its being most encouraging to me as a writer, what keeps returning to my mind is the moment of hearing I was to be in it. News of *Journey* inclusion came as the best kind of bizarre. A letter out of the blank blue of June, saying (in effect): We liked that story of yours so much we want to give it another airing in a special book, along with a dozen or so others. You'll be in excellent company. We'll send a cheque to cover the cost of an excellent single malt to celebrate. Oh, and we're going to give one of you ten thousand dollars. . . . All RIGHT! That wonderful postal moment is the essence of it, for me."   – Mike Barnes

"Way back in 1989, I got lucky with my first published story when it was selected for the *Journey Prize* anthology. Then I got lucky three more times. It is astounding to see how many writers published in the anthology over the last fifteen years have gone on to publish great story collections and novels. The anthology is a windfall for both writer and reader."

– David Bergen

"A great jolt of electricity startles the heart and jump-starts the writing career when you get the nod from the Journey people. It's a thrill to find your name included amongst some of the leading new voices in short fiction."   – Dennis Bock

"I had only just recognized my story 'Wave' as the seed of a novel when I learned it would be included in the prestigious *Journey Prize* anthology. The news thrilled me and, most importantly, came just when I craved a boost for the huge and scary task of shaping a novel. Once published, the anthology gave my work more exposure than it had ever had before, and continues to introduce new, innovative writers to a wider audience."

– Kristen den Hartog

"The name is felicitous, the company excellent, the honour ongoing. To have a story selected for the *Journey Prize* anthology at the beginning of one's publishing life is like being given

a lucky charm for the uncertain journey ahead. It opens doors (and eyes), provides encouragement and solace when needed, and offers assurance that there are indeed those who value the effort and artistry involved. This marvellous annual collection heralds and celebrates exciting new talent, and lets that talent know a steadily growing audience is waiting, and listening."
– Terry Griggs

"What a thrill! A yes instead of a no. I had done something right, and now I would have to figure out what it was."
– Elizabeth Hay

"I remember feeling ratified, authenticated, which of course was an illusion; no journal or anthology or prize ever proves you a real writer (whatever that is). But being chosen for an important anthology like the *Journey Prize* gave me a lift when I especially needed one, and I think of that with gratitude, admiration."
– Steven Heighton

"The writing apprenticeship is a long one, perhaps never-ending, and an appearance in the *Journey Prize* anthology is a boost of encouragement along the way. I am especially pleased that several of my former students have been included. Bravo for continuing to celebrate this challenging and exact genre – the story in its short form."   – Frances Itani

"The telegram, the telephone call, the electric jolt of a shot at $10,000 for a story and a banner unfurling in your brain. What are the odds? Very good odds, an antidote to discouraging words, to be acknowledged, a visitation in the boondock wilderness – no one knows you – hidden deep in the gymnasium's wallflower shadows and asked to dance. You step forward. The telegram, the telephone ringing, an electric jolt, and you float over the provinces, tickled pink as your map of Canada."
– Mark Anthony Jarman

"Being in the *Journey Prize* anthology – alongside all those other cakewalking babies – emboldened me enough to feel I could keep pursuing the kind of stories I really wanted to tell. Each year's anthology is like a kind of boulevard of promise, with the bright lights of so many fully developed, book-length works to come – by interesting, gifted writers – winking just up the road."

– Elise Levine

"Seeing my story 'Lessons from the Sputnik Diner' in the pages of the *Journey Prize* anthology was unforgettable. As a young writer, to be included in any anthology is something. To be chosen for a prestigious anthology that's featured writers whom you recognize and admire gives you quite a buzz. To know you are part of something that's become an institution in Canadian literature, providing an early venue for writers who often go on to be forces in the creative and imaginary life of this country, that's even further up a joyous road. Even if you are not famil-iar with its origins, there's no better name for the prize than Journey."

– Rick Maddocks

"In a matter of a few years, the *Journey Prize* anthology has become the proving ground for new, young Canadian writers, a who's who of the coming generation. You've been published in this and that literary review, great – but have you been published in the *Journey Prize* anthology? For many young writers (myself included), it's their first appearance in a 'real' book by a 'real' pub-lisher. After that, letters from editors get a lot more polite, even if they're rejections. The *Journey Prize* anthology is important to young writers because it is unique. There's nothing else like it in Canada. Writers who are 'big,' 'established,' 'older,' 'mature' – whatever you want to call them – have a panoply of prizes to honour them. . . . But for young writers, it's the Journey Prize or nothing. . . . I, for one, owe everything to the Journey Prize; I don't mean the money – I mean the attention, the publicity, the boost in confidence. . . . For obvious reasons, I remember the Journey Prize with fondness. It got the ball rolling for me."

– Yann Martel

"Congratulations on the fifteenth anniversary of the *Journey Prize* anthology. Inclusion of one of my stories – an excerpt from my novel-in-progress *Your Mouth Is Lovely* – was a source of great encouragement to me and a real thrill as well. Writing is always a solitary endeavour but at the beginning of a writing career it is also often an isolated one. There is no guarantee, ever, that a writer's work will be read and recognized, and as a beginning writer there are many moments of self-doubt in this regard. Inclusion in the *Journey Prize* anthology was invaluable to me in terms of the encouragement and boost in morale that it offered me. I have to add that I also appreciate the *Journey Prize* anthology as a reader. I buy it every year and read it cover to cover with great pleasure and interest. My thanks to McClelland & Stewart for publishing it, and may it be with us for many years to come."

– Nancy Richler

"I remember buying twenty copies of the fourth *Journey Prize* anthology, and giving them out to family for Christmas with my story helpfully Post-it marked. I finally got up the courage to ask a cousin what he thought of it, and he said, 'Yeah. It was long. Didn't finish it.' Which seemed to be the reaction of most of my family, except for my mom and dad, who kept their copy on the coffee table. The press and the attention I received from being in the anthology were important to my career, but not as crucial as my family finally referring to me as The Writer instead of The Most Educated Bum in Kitamaat Village." – Eden Robinson

"When the Journey Prize was established in 1989, I recall reading a *Globe and Mail* article about the first winner, Holley Rubinsky. I never thought I'd have a short story included in the

Journey Prize anthology eight years later. The door that opened for me in 1997 – one I imagined was a huge, locked door that might have been custom-made for the gods in Valhalla – stayed open. And I'm still a bit amazed that the door opened and that it has remained open since then."   – Anne Simpson

"Quite a few years before I would have dared call myself a writer in public, while I was still working at a bank, I began to buy the *Journey Prize* anthology yearly. I did so because I understood it to collect the best new short fiction of the year, and I hoped quietly that I would be inspired. One afternoon, a colleague caught me reading the anthology at my desk. Knowing a little about my literary interests, he asked bluntly: Are you in it this year? I wasn't, and I said so. But after he left my office, I remember my astonishment, my disbelief at his suggestion. These are 'real' writers (I wanted to shout), and while I aspire in the same direction, I have yet to publish a single story! About eight years later, I was included in the anthology and I remembered my colleague. It occurred to me that – despite the years I'd been at it and the stories that had since been published – nothing up to that point had convinced me that I could be a real writer. And while I remained astonished to see my name in those pages, the *Journey Prize* anthology now marked a beginning in which I could really believe. I've continued to read the anthology, and count it as an honour to have adjudicated during its fifteenth year. To me, its ongoing contribution is found on every page: new writers, new voices, new confidence."

– Timothy Taylor

"'Simple Recipes' was my first published story, and the one that, to my utter amazement, made it into the *Journey Prize* anthology. I remember getting the phone call, and remember sitting on the couch for a long time staring at the wall. I had a strange sense of vertigo, to think that it might actually be possible to one day write a book, and for that book one day to find readers. I had always quietly hoped for that possibility, but hadn't really thought about it within the boundaries of reality until that day."

– Madeleine Thien

"After a decade of writing fiction, I find to my amazement that the greatest imaginative feat required of me thus far has been the conception of myself as a writer. Every published story helped, but the day I learned my work was to be included in the eleventh volume of the *Journey Prize* anthology – and thereby in a national tradition of literary discovery – was the day when the writer I had long been imagining finally began to seem real."

– Alissa York

INTRODUCTION

The short story has never before been as flexible as it is today. There is an enormous and at times daunting scope of possibility within this famously difficult prose form. As a result, what makes a short story succeed – what makes it captivating and yet effortless, inventive and yet truthful – is not a matter that can be easily stated in summary.

Conventionally, the challenge of the short story seemed to be an issue of selective compression. The writer collapsed the world down to a fragment of its natural action and lined up views of character through the narrowest possible windows. By doing so with precision, a paradoxically complete vision of the world and its people was offered. The universe, in effect, expanded outward off the page, refracting through the tiny aperture of the story as if in adherence to some counterintuitive literary law of physics.

Of course, short stories still do this kind of thing. The 2003 Journey Prize jury read eighty-nine stories in the process of selecting those in this volume, and we encountered many that succeeded (some magnificently, we submit) in capturing the universe in precisely this fashion. But we also encountered stories that won us over quite differently. There were stories that teased with a half-hidden idea. Stories that spun threads of fantasy through concrete reality. Stories written in the manner of folk tales and others in unrelenting, unmediated vernacular. In short, we the jury – composed of three writers whose work is quite different from one another's – were delighted to find such diverse and original material, more evidence that the short-story form is evolving in exciting and unexpected ways – reflective in some measure, we thought, of the goings-on in the contemporary world at large.

From the eighty-nine disparate stories, each of which boasted individual accomplishments, here are the twelve stories that most captured us. Stories that nourished the imagination and provoked the intellect. From the hovering darkness in "Hush" to the existential jitters at play beneath the surface of "Conversion Classes." From the simultaneous warmth and cool of "Hansel and Gretel" to the spare perfection of "My Husband's Jump," in which both a character and a story take flight and do not touch down. These stories are examples of the powerful creative forces surging in the imaginations of some very talented writers.

We'd like to thank McClelland & Stewart for its commitment to bringing new writers to national attention each year. And a great debt of gratitude is also owed – by writers and readers – to the editors and staff of the many literary magazines in Canada who champion new work.

Michelle Berry
Timothy Taylor
Michael Winter
Toronto, April 2003

The Journey Prize Stories

S.K. JOHANNESEN

Resurrection

Mary Colavito, crippled in one of her feet from birth, grew up in a noisy and violent family in Camden, New Jersey, and ran away as soon as she could to an uncle, a sign-painter in Philadelphia. This sign-painter uncle was also a part-time pornographer who kept in his basement a large wooden camera and several lights on stands, with some simple props, and a darkroom, and sometimes put Mary in his pictures. Mary kept one of these pictures under the paper liner in the bottom drawer of her dresser because it was art and because she was in it.

She taught herself to play the piano from a book, on a battered upright with a broken player mechanism that her uncle had tuned for her and used sometimes as a prop in his pictures.

Mary's uncle treated her with kindness, and even with deference, as an unfortunate creature whom he credited with spiritual gifts. He made no objection when she said she was moving back to Camden. Mary had just turned seventeen.

She went to live with a sister who had a small flat and said Mary could live there until she found work. Having taken some typing lessons with money her uncle had given her, Mary found a job in a trucking company typing waybills and figuring out the complicated rates for different sorts of goods, whether they were knocked flat, or were especially heavy, or had a lot of packing around them, so that she made herself indispensable. The drivers made her a sort of mascot and brought little things back for her from their travels.

She went with her sister to Pentecostal meetings in Cherry Hill that a man named Brother Albanese and his pretty wife, also named Mary, conducted in the gymnasium of a public school on Sundays and on Wednesday nights until they could build their own church. Brother Albanese's Mary could not play the piano, which was an oversight on Brother Albanese's part, but which in his case only made people smile because he had light-coloured curly hair and a sweet bow of a mouth, and dark eyes and a firm jaw with a stubborn beard that always showed, however much he shaved. Mary Colavito was a godsend to them. She quickly learned all the songs and the choruses and played the piano with increasing skill and with evangelical ferocity.

In the year of Mary Colavito's nineteenth birthday, Sister Patsy came for revival meetings to the Albanese's church in Cherry Hill, and opened up in Mary's heart a space that had not existed before and Mary knew good and evil and was filled with terror.

She asked Brother Albanese if Sister Patsy would see her, feeling that she needed permission, and Brother Albanese listened gravely, and interceded with Sister Patsy after the service. A time was set for the next day.

Mary took time off her job, which she had never done before, and set out early, walking the last ten blocks rather than riding the bus all the way, to where Brother and Sister Albanese lived above a radio repair shop, and where Sister Patsy occupied the small spare bedroom reserved for evangelists who came to Cherry Hill.

At the time arranged, Mary entered the building by a single cement step and a painted door with three panes of glass above, at the side of the radio repair shop, and climbed the stairs to the landing. She knocked on the door of the Albaneses' flat. A distant voice, clear and musical, said, "Come."

Mary stepped onto the linoleum of the bright little kitchen

where she had been many times before to play Parcheesi and drink cocoa with the Albaneses. Beyond the kitchen she could see the bare sitting room with its second-hand green velour sofa and two matching chairs, and beyond that, two bedrooms, the doors side by side, both of them open. At the far end of the smaller of these rooms, in a small chair with open arms, by the single window, sat Sister Patsy. She motioned to Mary to approach.

The room had space only for a single metal bed, a yellow-stained plywood wardrobe, a white-painted table, and the chair in which Sister Patsy was sitting. Sister Patsy wore a plain white dress with white stockings and white shoes and a pink satin sash tied around her waist. Her hair was loose and clean and floated in the yellow light from the window at her side.

"Come sit here, Mary." Sister Patsy gestured toward the foot of the bed.

It was Autumn, and cold outside, and although it was warm in the room, Mary still shivered a little. She perched stiffly on the edge of the bed where Sister Patsy had pointed, her crippled foot not quite reaching the floor.

Sister Patsy said nothing more but waited, as though it were the most natural thing to receive a visitor in a bedroom, without taking her things, or offering her coffee, or making her comfortable.

Mary snuffled, and hugged herself and rocked to and fro. She stood then, crookedly, her coat still about her, her hat now awry, and looked at the wall. She reached in the pocket of her coat with a gloved hand and took out a stiff card, about four by six inches, and handed it to Sister Patsy without looking at her.

Mary Colavito collapsed back on to the bed, and half-lay, twisted sideways, an arm over her face, quietly sobbing.

Sister Patsy looked at the picture.

A man is sitting on a chair. He sits far forward and is leaning back. He wears socks and garters, and a woman's bloomers, open in the crotch, the draw-strings trailing below.

A woman, naked, straddles him, her back to the camera, her face hidden. Her unruly hair, partly held with a dark ribbon, conceals the man's face.

She is plump; folds of fat run diagonally across her back. Her buttocks are high, perfectly round, very white and smooth. The camera is placed low and permits us to see her sex in the sharpest detail. A glistening cleft, like a marine creature, dark hair descending abundantly on either side, as much vegetable as animal, like Spanish moss, or like the beard of a god.

The delicate fringes of her sex clasp the end of the man's penis, the base part of which is visible above large round testicles in a smooth and nearly hairless scrotum. The penis is thick and tapered, strained taut against the angle by which it is seized, corded veins standing out on its surface like ivy on a beech tree in winter.

On the left side of the woman stands Mary Colavito, slight and dark, a serious and compressed face below a narrow monkey-brow, looking downward, toward the camera, an arrangement of leaves on her head, a white shift covering her from her breasts to her hips. Her legs and feet are bare and her deformed foot on its wasted leg is raised on a low stool, in white relief against the darkest part of the background. Her hand rests delicately, without weight, on the woman's near buttock, her thumb and middle finger together in a mysterious gesture of benediction, or perhaps of creative power.

This hand, its attitude and placement, more than anything else, governs the mood of the entire tableau, which is suspended motion, everything moulded as though in wax, yet not dead or frozen, but glowing from within with nerveless vitality.

Sister Patsy looked at the photograph for a long time.

At last she got up from her chair and placed the photograph on the white table, face up, in the exact centre of the table, as though this placement were important. She turned to Mary Colavito on the bed, now quiet, still half lying, her legs dangling over the edge. Sister Patsy loosened the hair pins that held Mary's crushed hat, and put the hat on the far side of the narrow bed. She lifted Mary's legs, with the black laced-up boots still on, the normal one and the one built up because of her foot, and laid them carefully on the white candlewick coverlet. Then she pulled her chair closer to the bed and sat in it again and took the glove off the hand that wasn't covering Mary's face, and held the hand in both of her own, and after a long interval began to speak softly.

"Where I grew up," Sister Patsy began, "in a place far from here, there were many pigs. Long narrow ones with pink ears and white hair on their backs. I gave names to them, from the Bible. There was Bathsheba of course, and Sapphira, and Deborah, and Rebecca, and the boy pigs were mostly kings. Two of these I especially loved. They were kept in a separate pen, and Mr. Shoemaker was particular that they had shade for the hottest days, and a bit of mud to roll in but not too much, and a place that was dry, with straw, to lie down in.

"I called one of them Jeroboam, for he had a crafty and rebellious nature and loved the mud and rolled his eye in a dangerous way, which made me think of that king of Israel who loved the high places. While the other one, whom I named Rehoboam, had a sweeter nature, and kept himself clean, and was trusting, and made me think of God's promise to save Judah, for the sake of King David, the sweet singer of Israel. I also remembered that King Rehoboam, although he was not as wise as his father Solomon, was descended from Ruth, who gleaned in the fields with Naomi and lay at the feet of Boaz.

"One day Rehoboam died. Mrs. Shoemaker thought we shouldn't leave him in the pen, because Jeroboam would eat him and perhaps also become sick and die. She said it couldn't wait for Mr. Shoemaker to come home.

"She backed the tractor up to the pen, and we tied a rope around Rehoboam's feet and the other end around the bar on the back of the tractor, and she dragged Rehoboam through a gate into a field of stubble, and I walked behind.

"We went through that field and into another that was a meadow but there were no sheep or cows in it at that time of year. At the far end of the field there were rocks, white, rounded rocks that looked like sheep themselves, and at one place the rocks rose into a little hill with a thicket of honey locusts at the top, which were covered with the longest thorns you'd ever seen, even all around the trunks. And around behind the thicket was a bare patch of dirt among the rocks that had been dug up by woodchucks, or maybe a dog that was after them, because there was a very large hole that went into the hill under the honey locusts.

"We put Rehoboam in the hole as best we could, which was only part way in. But he was concealed from every direction except the sky, because of the rocks and the honey locusts, and a fence with a line of willows on the other side."

As Sister Patsy told her story, the arm that covered Mary's face relaxed a bit at a time, uncovering first one ear, and then one eye. She was silent, and listening intently. Sister Patsy paused, shifted herself in her chair, and continued.

"That night we told Mr. Shoemaker what we did, and he sighed and scratched his ear, and went out on the porch, the way he always did.

"After that I went over toward the hill nearly every day. I peeked whenever I dared. At first it was just flies, and Rehoboam swelled up so his feet stuck out. Then after about three days it stunk so bad all around the hill I had to hold my nose tight, and then it got even worse and I had to hold my breath and could only run up to take a peek and run away again. The crows and the buzzards came. You could see them circling high in the air, and they would get closer and closer, and disappear behind the honey locusts. If I got too close they would flap their wings and rise up a bit, and squawk. And at night there were the skunks. There was an extra smell in the morning that meant they had been there.

"After a week of this, the stink died down, and the birds went away. I went over to have a good look. Rehoboam was mostly yellow bones and patches of skin, some of it still with the hair on, and the skull and the backbone were picked but not completely, and there were maggots in them.

"I ran down by the fence and found a stick and some willow branches, and I pushed what was left of Rehoboam a little further into the hole, and swished the branches around in the dirt to hide that the birds and the skunks had been there and to make it all clean. Then I moved a flat rock that was nearby that wasn't too heavy and partly covered the hole with it and laid the branches I had over that. It was like a little grave.

"The Church of the Brethren that I was raised with didn't think that animals had souls and never thought to pray for them, and so I didn't either, but I sang a song for Rehoboam that was one of our old songs in German that I didn't understand, but it was slow and mournful.

"I didn't return to Rehoboam's grave for a while. I waited until a Sunday morning a week or two later, and was up before Mr. and Mrs. Shoemaker. I had my Sunday dress on, and best shoes, but I pulled some old galoshes of Mrs. Shoemaker's over them, and raced over the fields to have a look. I pulled back the branches, which were wilted now, and I could see over the top of the stone I had put there, and shielded my eyes and waited until I could see properly into the dark hole.

"Rehoboam was gone. Just as I knew he would be. I looked some more and squinted, to be absolutely sure. I sniffed in the hole and there was nothing but a dry smell, like root vegetables kept in a cellar for the winter, or the smell of caterpillars when you keep them in a coffee can. It was as though he had never been there. I ran home and started breakfast for Mr. and Mrs. Shoemaker, and pretended nothing had happened."

Sister Patsy shifted again, and looked at the yellow-stained wardrobe. "That was the only thing I ever kept from them."

"Why did you keep it from them?" said Mary Colavito in a muffled voice, in spite of herself.

The sun had been sinking and now shone into the room below the blind and threw a mantle of liquid gold over the two women.

"Because –"

Sister Patsy thought for a moment.

"Because that belonged to me. I wasn't hurting them by not telling them. I would have hurt myself a lot if I had. Rehoboam wouldn't have come to me again."

"He came to you?" Mary had now turned her face full on Sister Patsy.

"Oh, yes," said Sister Patsy.

"He was a king, you see. Whenever I saw him he had on a red coat, with gold braid and buttons, very proud, but sad in his eyes, because he remembered everything. He remembered that he had died, and he remembered the vultures and the other animals that tore at his body and left him nothing but rotting skin.

"But not any more," said Sister Patsy after a sigh. "I don't see him now. He has gone for good."

Sister Patsy helped Mary to her feet and wiped her eyes and helped her blow her nose into the hanky that she took from her sash, and collected Mary's hat and gloves. Then she got the photograph from the table and put it in Mary's pocket and kissed her face tenderly.

"Do not give up anything of yourself until you know what it has to teach you," Sister Patsy said.

Shortly after these events in Camden, Sister Patsy went to Brooklyn to be pastor of Eben-ezer. The next year Mary Colavito rang, having asked her landlady to let her use the phone. Her landlady agreed, on the condition that Mary get the operator to ring her back with the charges. When she got Sister Patsy on the phone – the landlady listening in to see she was not cheated – Mary said she wanted to come to New York. Sister Patsy said she could use a good pianist in Eben-ezer. Mary said goodbye to Brother and Sister Albanese and to her sister, and packed her few things.

They had a party for her at the shipping office, and the boss gave her the name of a trucking company in Brooklyn. He wrote a note and said give this to Max, and tell Max he owes Sid in Camden one, and tell him to look out for you kid. When the time came to leave, one of the drivers going to New England took her in the cab with him and said he would drop her off safe and sound, which he did, all the way to New York, through the Holland Tunnel and over the Manhattan Bridge and up Flatbush Avenue to Fourth Avenue and right to the door of Eben-ezer.

CHARLOTTE GILL

Hush

Brian loves Patty in a quiet, sublime sort of a way, always has. He feels lucky, exempt from the marital cycles of jagged passion and boredom. But lately? He hears her shoes on the steps and his ass clenches. Since his *accident*, as he likes to think of it, or perhaps even before, there's been something new. He listens to the long, belaboured pause between the key and the door and her arrival, like nothing in the world is easy. He struggles off the couch, slaps the TV off on the way to the hall, where he greets her with a kiss on the forehead. He makes a feeble play for the grocery bags dangling at her wrists. She wears the trench coat and the Reeboks – a uniform that makes him lose track of the days.

For dinner they are going to have steamed organic spinach with roasted sesame seeds and strands of seaweed that look like little black shoelaces. Patty expresses her mood in some snippy chopping and peeling of vegetables. They are going to eat marinated slabs of tofu, baked on a cookie sheet. Puréed organic parsnip.

At the table he asks, "Is there butter?"

"Butter's full of toxins." She passes him chopsticks. "But you can have applesauce for dessert."

Brian can handle the wacky diet. They have a nice life. They have no children and no plans for children, which is all right since neither one of them can see the point of the constant, low-level chaos. He can handle the tired sighs and the miserable tilt to her eyebrows and the things she almost says but doesn't.

They eat in silence. It passes for appreciation.

After dinner, they do what they always do. She washes. He dries. "Look," he says. He nudges her with his elbow and points to the window.

Patty's hands leave the sink. She steals his dishtowel away.

They huddle at the window together. A snotty evening rain runnels down the glass, obscuring their view of a little round woman trundling up the driveway. She carries a blanketed bundle in one arm, holds her jacket over her head with the other.

"That's the wife," Brian murmurs.

"Look who's been spying." The dishtowel is like a tongue between Patty's folded arms.

"With a baby."

"Uh-oh," she says.

"So far the husband's a putz."

"If we're going to peep," says Patty, "shouldn't we turn off the light?"

Brian watches dating shows back-to-back, the California bozos with capped teeth and the pretty girls with their superior tits. Patty is too pure for all this. But she knits by his side – another Christmas present, another non-surprise he'll try not to wear beyond the driveway. She creeps off her armchair when he's not looking. He notices her absence, slides off the couch, and goes looking.

He finds her hiding behind the bathroom door, already deep into stage one of the complicated oral hygiene regimen that doubles as a means of keeping him – and sex – at bay. By the time she's finished he'll be down on the pillow, turning out the lights in his mind. So he barges in. He watches her spread antibacterial goop on each of her front teeth, then go at the molars with a miniature gumline brush. She looks at him and scrubs harder. Brian plucks the toothbrush from her mouth. "How are you feeling?" he asks.

"Terrible," she says. Her mouth is full of suds. "But it has nothing to do with you."

When they get into bed, Patty flips from her side to her front, cramming and prodding the pillow underneath her until it's satisfactorily positioned. Brian lies flat on his back.

The doors get locked. The cars in the neighbourhood get parked in their slots. His body winds down. He falls asleep. She falls asleep. The world relaxes. But not tonight. There's something underneath the deep rumble of the furnace and the sigh of their breath. Downstairs the baby is crying. "Oh," Patty groans. She buries her head under the duvet. "Here we go."

The alarm clock goes off like an air horn, slicing through Patty's half-sleep. She drags herself from the blankets, stands on the rug watching Brian, his face collapsed in sleep. For a second she thinks about stuffing his open mouth with the corner of her pillow. But she doesn't. She showers and dresses. She feeds herself breakfast and hauls herself down to the car like a great burlap sack of salt with a hole torn in the bottom.

Outside the sky is a big grey pancake with pink light sizzling at its distant edges. She gets into her Honda. She lets it take her to the exit and onto the highway that feeds itself over the bridge. When it comes time to signal and nudge her way into the downtown core, she could just keep driving into the mountains. Too bad there's nothing out there but antipodal cravings, nothing in between but deer and rednecks.

At work, she's the first. The office is deserted. It has the feeling of a surprise party that no one's remembered. She cloisters herself in the corner cubicle where she earns a non-union wage as a tertiary assistant in the tertiary world of HR. On the middle of her desk blotter rests a mussed tower of paper and files. It's hackled with Post-its.

"Go to hell, Wanda," says Patty to the stack.

The phone twitters and she jumps. These days any little thing makes her start. Her hand trembles out to answer it. "Hello?" she says.

"Robin?" It's the man with the creamy, intelligent voice. "Robin Brothers?"

"Didn't you phone me yesterday?" Patty asks.

"No," he says.

"Are you sure? Very, very sure?"

"Totally," he says.

"Well," she sighs, "I'm still not Robin."

"Wrong number," he says and hangs up.

The other girls begin to arrive. *Hello*, they sing to one another. They change their shoes. *Good morning.*

Patty has a recurring daydream of an anonymous man who makes love to her in a nice hotel room with open windows and white curtains while men shout foreign curses in the street below. Who is this man, her nameless, faceless, perfect mate? The weatherman? The man with the intelligent voice? It doesn't matter. She looks for him wherever she goes.

Such thoughts are a horrible waste of time, Patty admits. Perhaps what she needs is a *real* affair. So she can lie like a chromosome, her X to a strange Y on a strange bed with sheets that smell of bleach. So she can wonder who else has screwed furtively or jerked off to porn or perhaps died on the mattress that holds her in its overused trough. Maybe what she needs is something that ends badly.

Patty shoves away from her desk and stands up. Her co-workers sit at their stations, a coven of typing and clicking. Patty stalks down to Wanda's door. She knocks and enters, finds Wanda at her desk surrounded by symmetrical document piles. At her elbow, a giant Starbucks cup with lipstick smeared on the lid.

"I'm not feeling well," says Patty.

Wanda squints at her. "You're kidding. These binders have to go out by three." Wanda is a lean triathlete bitch with smart

angular glasses and an angular body that performs like an infal-
libly well-tuned machine.

"I'm feeling awful," says Patty, "and I'd hate to spread it around."

A week ago, on his rounds, he emptied an ATM in a convenience
store. One of the neighbourhood street freaks decided to hook
him in the nuts, for no reason at all, with a full bottle of Sprite.
Until yesterday he could barely walk. The doctor called it *acute
contusion* and prescribed medication for the pain. But pills do
nothing for his pride. They don't stop his Brinks buddies from
calling to hassle him. "She gotcha good, didn't she?"

"To tell the truth," Brian says, "I couldn't tell if it was a she
or a he."

For now he's laid up at home, dribbling water into the house-
plants according to Patty's detailed instructions. The kitchen
window looks out onto the backyard, the driveway, and the
lane, and he watches a gang of guys budge a huge sectional out
of a cube van. They'll try to squeak it through the basement
door into the suite downstairs. They'll fail, he can see that
right now. Someone will come up and knock. Someone who
doesn't speak English. They'll want to heave it through Brian's
upstairs apartment and go down through the laundry room.
Brian will have to agree to watch them ding the drywall and
shuffle along on the clean carpet in their dirty boots. Or maybe
he'll just say no. The couch belongs to their new downstairs
neighbours, who are foreigners.

The former tenant was an old unmarried carpenter from when
the neighbourhood was German. He lived in the suite beneath
Brian and Patty, off a pension and odd jobs. He didn't smoke or
flush at night or run his tools in the house. He didn't have girlfriends. He fixed things that needed fixing. But then he died, and
that was the end of a very good thing.

The waiting room is lavishly perfumed with lavender, a scent
associated in her mind with her doctor, who wears no lab coat

and asks that her patients call her Yasmin. Her inner office is unlike any other doctor's office. There are ferns, fig plants, and a Wandering Jew. The walls are the colour of sand. There are ambient nature sounds to choose from: Surf, Breeze, or Babbling Brook.

"I'm always awake." Patty lies back on the table, which is more like a couch than a table. "Even when I'm asleep."

"I know," says Yasmin, who doctors with a firm, clean hand. "You've said." She begins by probing the arch of Patty's left foot with an electronic pen that reads the state of her insides. Patty stares at the ceiling, nervous about her liver. The machine bleats.

"What does that mean?" Patty wants to know.

"It means you can't tolerate caffeine. Caffeine is full of toxins."

"But I don't drink coffee."

"Then it must be something else."

"What?"

"Don't worry," says Yasmin. "We'll find out."

After the session Yasmin escorts Patty to the waiting room, where she jots things down for the receptionist. She invites the next clients in – a thin, pimply boy and his mother. How vigorous and healthy Yasmin looks by comparison, what perfect skin. Patty wants that skin.

The receptionist fetches two brown dropper bottles from the refrigerator, then slides them over the counter along with a sheet of paper, still warm from the printer. Patty's eyes skim over the numbers and columns to the bottom right-hand corner – the total registers like a dizzying height. She presses her hand to her breastbone. "Is this right?" she asks. The receptionist nods and brandishes a pen. Patty takes out her cheques. She signs her wavy name on the straight line and rips the cheque out of the book.

Ever since moving in, the guy downstairs comes out of his apartment between ten and noon with a white plastic grocery bag full of garbage. He dangles it at arm's-length by the rabbit-eared handles as if he's not well acquainted with trash. He walks out to the lane and drops it into the garbage can. Then the guy – Brian has learned he goes by "Joe" (too Anglo, it's suspicious) though they have not yet met – scans up the alley and down the alley from under the duck bill of his ball cap. Then he goes inside.

Today there is no garbage, but two of Joe's buddies roll up in a red Mustang convertible. The driver wears a silver down jacket, though the day is unseasonably warm. The other, a Grizzlies sweatshirt with a hood and cut-off sleeves. Both wear sunglasses and shitty little goatees. They honk the horn and Joe saunters out in Nike shoes worth two hundred bucks, a cellphone pressed to his ear. The guy in the front passenger seat gets out and leaps over the door into the back. Joe gets in next to the driver. The muffler farts out clouds of white smoke. The driver leans forward to retrieve something from the glovebox, obscuring Brian's view of Joe. Then whatever is happening has happened. Joe gets out and heads back to his apartment. The Mustang rumbles away, the muffler like the roll of a big fat snare. Brian writes down the licence plate number on the back of his hand.

Drugs, drive-by shootings, B and Es. Brian concerns himself with these things. He has worked in security since he was seventeen years old. He has worked. He's put in his sweat and his toil. Now he's more than twice seventeen, and his neighbourhood is evolving for the worse. He's not surprised. Entropy is the rule of the cosmos. Events begin well with a few surmountable complications. A taken-for-granted cresting. Then there's the inevitable downhill slide before everything begins to decay. He can think of nothing in life that's exempt from this pattern except for cockroaches and plastic. Nothing important, anyway. Neighbourhoods. Governments, empires, alliances. Buildings and other edifices. Everything goes to shit. Species with no natural predators. Polar ice caps. Bones and teeth and skin. Snowmen. Beauty. Rock bands. Marriage. Love.

Patty walks in. She's early, unexpected. She takes a look at him on the bed and asks, "How's your acute contusion?"

Who puts the cogs back in the universe once all the springs have sprung?

Brian steps down off the bed and lands with a thud on the carpet.

"What else do you get up to when I'm gone?" she wants to know. Patty is a Capricorn, all business about feelings until they're her own. She's still in her coat holding a fistful of keys.

"I keep on top of the highlights," he says darkly.

"What else?"

"Is this a quiz?"

Patty sighs. She brushes her bangs aside, then lets her arm slap down against her handbag. She inserts one of her keys into the niche in the door jamb. She digs around, and sawdust falls to the carpet like dandruff.

"Why are you doing that?" he asks.

She stops. "Did you go down and mention the crying?"

"I went down," he lies. "But there was nobody home."

She pinches her lips to one side. She holds up the end of her scarf, looks at it intently, folds it in half, then in half again.

Patty sweeps out the back door and hustles down the stairs. With each step she charts out what she will say and not say to these neighbours downstairs. The baby is not yet crying, but it will, later, when she's in bed, because that's what babies do. Babies need to be wiped and cleaned. They scream and insist. They undo their mothers in public. All that tyrannical, reflexive want packaged up inside something so small and deceptively cute. But it's not the baby she can't stand. It's dependency, help-lessness. It's Brian.

She knocks. The door is flung open and Joe appears, looking like a big, neckless bouncer. Patty takes a hesitant step back. "I'm wondering –" she begins, but Joe has disappeared. Patty is left gazing at a pile of big shoes and little shoes on the square of linoleum that separates the laundry room from their neigh-bours' low-ceilinged zone. Inside the apartment there's a cascade of syllables she can't understand. The smell of onions frying in butter. Where have all these shoes come from? It could be anywhere between Turkey and Bangladesh for all she knows.

Patty hears the swish of legs, nylon against nylon. The wife appears in bare feet, a navy-blue Gap T-shirt and warm-up pants. There's a palm-print of flour under the A and the P on her shirt.

Patty has it all lined up in her mind. She's going to convey her complaint monosyllabically and with gestures. But Patty finds herself forgetting her purpose. She's struck by how young and pretty and round the wife is. She says her own name again and pats herself on the chest.

"Karam," says the wife.

"Karam," Patty repeats. From now on she will want to get it mixed up with *karma*. "Your baby," Patty begins. Despite her intentions, these words leak out sounding accusatory or portentous. Karam's brow furrows. She squares herself in preparation for bad news or complaint. She looks used to bad news and complaints.

It's going to be tougher than Patty thought, this fine line between simplicity and condescension – when you don't speak each other's language, everyone ends up feeling stupider. Patty makes a cradle of her arms. Karam smiles edgily, revealing white, white teeth that have never seen coffee or tea. Before Patty can say more, Karam, too, slips from sight, leaving Patty to wait on the step again.

Karam returns, the nylon rustling softly this time, with the baby in a yellow sleeper. She holds it up for Patty as a testament to its inarguable cuteness. Only the baby isn't pretty. "Oh," says Patty. She leans in closer. It has a big lolling tongue and pointed lips. Shiny, purplish eyelids. It looks like a little brown turtle. A turtle with no shell.

Patty had things organized in her mind. She was going to explain that she is a very light sleeper. That she can't do without sleep. That sleep is the most fundamental aspect of good health. But all the fight has drained out of her. "Oh, my," says Patty, touching its sharp fingernails. Fingernails the size of crumbs. Is it sick? Is it mentally deformed? She's forgotten all her lines.

Brian eases bare-chested into sheets as crisp and knife-edged and as comfortable as parchment.

Patty flips the clasps on her jewelry. "There's something wrong with that baby."

"Well, there's nothing wrong with its lungs."

"It doesn't look right." Now she peels off the turtleneck. Underneath it is the familiar beige-toned bra with the wide straps and the mysterious closure.

"Well, what?"

She shrugs.

With habitual coyness, she turns away as if she's got a kind of virginity left to keep from him, something not yet seen. She thinks her inner thighs are starting to sag. As if he doesn't already know about her thighs or the pouch of flab around her navel. "Did you mention the thinness of our floors?"

The hem of the nightie flutters down past her shoulders and hips. "I never got that far."

"You lost your nerve."

She flashes on him. "Why are you bugging me?"

"I'm not."

"I had a language barrier to contend with."

"So you point at the baby and cover your ears."

"Why don't *you* point and cover your ears."

This used to be his favourite part of the day. He used to watch Patty shuck off her clothes and her day and think: This woman is my mate. I want to impregnate this person. I want to be worth a million bucks. I want to crawl inside her as if she were a cupboard and taste everything inside.

They stopped sleeping naked after Patty read a book by a doctor from Colorado. According to the book, shoes were a bad idea and bras were a good idea. Sleeping naked was also bad because it disrupted your circadian cycle. For years she'd been turning over, waking herself up with blasts of cold air.

"So sleep closer," Brian said.

When she climbs into bed he fields her like a giant baseball mitt. She fidgets in his embrace. She's used to Brian on night shift, used to sleeping in the middle of the bed. Does she really want to feel the course hair on his thigh? Does he really want to feel her cold ass at his hip? Sleeping naked is for other people, couples still fascinated with each other's bodies, for those who can overlook the ingrown stubble and the midnight farts.

She's no fan of the human body, it's true. There are too many ways to get sick. There's a certain type of micro-organism that dwells only on eyelashes. A zillion kinds of bacteria in her gut. Everyday all the earth's fungal spores rain down on her body. Sometimes she hates her own skin. Sometimes she can't scrub hard enough.

"I don't hear anything," she says. "Do you?"

He grunts, disgustingly half-asleep.

"You're too hot," she says, shoving off from him.

She lies awake staring at the darkness, listening to his breath descend into the deep, familiar rasps of a snore. No one ever died because of lack of sleep? She's read experiments on sleep deprivation in rats. After three days with no sleep they claw and tear at each other's fur. After a week they burrow into their corners and lie there inert.

A few streets away, a siren dopplers by and her whole body tenses. It's not the crying baby itself, but the *idea* of a crying baby, the proximity of stress and discomfort, the *waiting*, that shreds the quiet in her mind. Brian sleeps, oblivious. The siren sets the rotten dog howling behind the fence next door. Patty holds her breath. When the crying begins, it's no surprise. It travels up from the basement, up the stairwell, and through the rooms of their apartment and into her ear canals. The wailing begins light and faint, then blossoms into waves of shrieking and gasping. Her mind follows the cadence, a lump of anger rising up in her throat. She pounces up on all fours. Brian turns onto his side and reaches for her shoulder. "Don't." She quivers on the verge of tears. "Don't even touch me."

The horizon pukes sherbety light on another shitty, gorgeous morning. Patty storms out of bed, throws her clothes on the bed, and stomps around on her heels over every square foot of the apartment. She feels like a stretched length of yarn, like something dangled from a rooftop. Brian appears, puffy-eyed. His big goofy hands scratch around in the pockets of his robe. "What's up?" he wants to know.

"I'm going to *work*." She looks at him through eye slits, on the verge of some dangerous honesty. She fumes into the hall and snatches her coat off its hook. Brian's slippers scuff along the floor. *Pick up your goddamn feet*, she thinks.

"Look," says Brian at the door to the basement, which is ajar. On the floor between the door and the jamb rests a palm-sized lump, wrapped in coloured cellophane. He nudges it with his toe, then picks it up. "This must be for you."

"How do you know?"

"It's pink, for a start."

She takes it out of his hands and yanks at the corkscrew of ribbon. The plastic comes apart. Inside are four white cakes, cut into the shapes of diamonds. She holds one to her nose and the smell is nearly indescribable: like rose petals, crushed and wet. But also something creamy and edible. It reminds her of something she can't quite place. Something lovely. From childhood.

"Is that soap?" Brian asks. "It looks like soap."

She peeks through the open door into the unlit stairwell and catches a whiff of another smell that isn't hers or Brian's, a smell that's decisively *theirs*. Without thinking, Patty lifts one to her mouth nibbles a corner. A milky sweetness floods over her tongue. Her eyes water – she hasn't had sugar in years. "It's not soap," she says. Though she'd rather it was.

Brian is basically happy. He wanders from room to room, forgetting his purpose. Perhaps all that's needed is a little air, some locomotion. He pokes his head through the neck hole of the Harvard sweatshirt – a gift from his mother, who trots off to all parts since the death of his father – as yet unworn. He slides his arms into it but then takes it off because only morons advertise the fact of their non-education. He's very happy and mostly optimistic, but the world has its lucent truths.

Outside the weather's fine. Sun-dappled sidewalks, a moist breeze. He begins at a careful stroll, assessing the status of his injury. All is fine. The neighbourhood rhododendrons bloom. The aroma of flowers is everywhere.

He proceeds to the park without deciding to. At the gates an old guy hurries a Yorkie down the asphalt path. "Come on, Rippy." Rippy sniffs and pees on the underbrush. "Rippy, let's go." The guy becomes resentful, yanks Rippy along in his harness. It's his wife's dog, obviously.

Brian quickens his pace to a vigorous walk. But three-quarters of the way around the path a knifing pain shoots through what he's sure must be his prostate.

He hobbles around the circuit in the requisite direction, perturbed by the pedestrian traffic. Suddenly everyone's annoying. The skateboard punks, the old dames, slow as ducks. *Get a job*, he wants to say to everyone he passes. Even the chatty girls with the high ponytails and the nice calves and the pompoms at the heels of their socks.

Brian limps back to the house. Upon arrival he finds Patty, back again early from work. She's cross-legged on the couch, staring at the sky beyond the window. No guy likes to see his wife in a meltdown – after all, it's probably his fault – but this is terrible. Patty's face leaks tears and mucus. His nuts throb with a vicious ache. He thinks of this pain as laden with meaning, there to punish or humble him in some medicinal, necessary way. Her hand clutches out at his, her fingers chilled and moist.

"Can't you hear it?" she asks.

The next thought that darts through his mind startles him: *What if she's gone crazy?* "I don't hear a thing." He crafts the sentence with his least offensive tone.

"Smell that," she says. "Do you smell that?" Patty has burst into the room where Brian wipes polish onto his workboots in slow, deliberate strokes.

He sniffs and shrugs.

"It's electrical." Her nose works the air like a marsupial's. "Like hot metal." Her eyes land on the blackened rag between his fingers, the boot between his knees. She gasps and rolls her eyes as if he's the most obtuse human being she's ever known. She whirls and flees the scene.

"That hurts," he says to the wall.

When the smoke detector starts to blare downstairs, she collides with him in the hallway. "Fire," she says, clutching him by the buttons and the chest hair. "They're trying to burn the house down." He disentangles her fingers but lets her drag him by the forearm down the basement steps to the laundry, where their downstairs neighbours have spread out an assortment of belongings. Brian and Patty walk the path of clear floor past the washing machine. Patty nudges things out of the way with the side of her foot and the back of her hand – satin blankets and underwear strung on clotheslines and garbage bags full of extra whatever.

Patty pounds on the door. Brian can see her thinking what she's already told him dozens of times: These are people who never throw things out. Who will never teach their child not to shriek for attention. Who believe in nylon and polyester and disposable diapers. Who sweep the floor but not the corners. They're those kind of people.

The door opens. Joe emerges in a black Gold's Gym T-shirt, yacking urgently into a cordless phone over the blast of the smoke alarm. Patty shoots Brian a look over her shoulder.

Brian sees they are exactly the same height. He can look Joe straight in the eye.

"Where is the fire?" Patty demands. The urgent authority in her voice makes Joe step aside. Patty attempts to dart past him into the house, but he stops her by the forearm and points down at her shoes. "Oh, give me a break," says Patty, kicking off her shoes in an exasperated rush.

In sock feet Brian steps into the apartment, which is different from what he remembers. Long tubes of fluorescent light and commercial-grade low-pile carpet, stone grey, the same as in the office where his supervisor and the dispatch girls work. Good for high traffic, stain resistance, rug burns.

A stratum of thin blue smoke hovers a foot from the ceiling. Patty zips instinctively into the kitchen. Brian follows her. Joe follows Brian. Patty scans the stove dials and pulls at the oven door. It won't open. "What's in here?" she yells at Joe. Joe shrugs. He's off the phone now but holds it in his hand. "What do you mean you don't know? Is your wife not home?" He pulls at his lower lip, guilty and bewildered. She points to a knob. "Do you know what you did? You put your pizza on self-clean. The door won't open until the cycle's done." She touches the stove with her finger, then withdraws it quickly. She makes a sizzling sound with her mouth.

Patty is formidable. "I think he understands the *hot* part," Brian says. Brian almost feels bad for Joe.

Patty turns to Brian. "Move it for me, Moose."

"What if I get electrocuted?" asks Brian. She hasn't called him Moose in ten years.

Patty sets her hand on the stove. "We'll get electrocuted together."

Joe slides into his wife's oven mitts. Brian wraps two dish towels around his hands. He touches the corner of the stove and breaks into an instant sweat. He and Joe grunt and jiggle and scrape the thing away from the wall.

When there's room Patty dives in behind it, wiggles her slight frame into the space they've made for her. Brian peers over the back where Patty, bent sideways at the waist, works the plug prongs back and forth. She stands up. "There." She drops the cord on the floor like a snake she's just strangled with her bare hands.

Brian and Joe stand there looking at each other as if they should shake hands. Patty bustles deeper into the apartment down the narrow strip of hallway. She stops in front of two closed doors under the smoke detector, which she's too short to reach. "Kill it," she shouts with her eyes closed, fingers in her ears.

Brian comes to her aid, reaches to the ceiling, and rips the cover off the smoke detector. He pulls the wire cap from the nine-volt. Joe sidles up behind them like a passerby. Brian glances at the leaping white cat and the bolt of lightning on the battery's casing, then hands it to Joe. Joe stares at it on the flat of his palm.

Patty turns the knob on one of the doors. The baby's cries blare out at them from the darkness. Patty steps into it. Brian's eyes adjust. Patty makes shushing noises on her way to the bed, a twin with a pillow wedged under the mattress to keep the baby from rolling out. She picks the baby up under the arms like a woman with no idea of how to proceed with such a task. She brings the baby out. It wears a white sleeper with pink elephants on it, joined in concentric chains by nose and trunk. It's head lolls and rolls in towards her neck but it does not stop crying. "You hold it," she says accusingly. She passes it off to Joe, who handles it like a bag of rolling potatoes. "You hold it. It stops crying. Simple."

Upstairs Patty flings open all the windows. Brian trails after her like a simpering boob from room to room so that she can't think straight. "That baby's going to cry until the end of time," she laments.

"It won't."

"We're going to go mad."

"We'll move."

"No way," she says, stomping her foot for emphasis. "We were here first."

"Well, we'll make sure and tell them that."

"You're no help at all."

He looks at her and sighs, "What do you want me to say? That the baby is crying on purpose just to piss you off?"

Patty throws her arms up in the air. They are back in the kitchen where they started. How should she know why babies cry? She doesn't have one. She and Brian are DINKs with the combined income of a veteran Safeway cashier. But why stop there? Here's to not going on vacations. Here's to renting, not buying. To their postal code. The White Spot. Rusty shitbox cars. Here's to Winners and Payless. No frills and bag lunches. Here's to no kids. To having run out of ways to amuse oneself.

Patty slings her purse onto the counter by the straps. She rifles through to the very bottom in search of her wallet.

Brian hovers at her side with the meat of his palm on the sink's edge.

"How much cash have you got?" she wants to know.

He slides his wallet out of his back pocket and counts out a few well-used, flannel-textured bills.

"What for?" he asks. "Are you planning to *buy* the baby?"

She nips at his money with the ends of her fingers. Brian holds it in the air just beyond her reach.

"Give it to me," says Patty.

"No," says Brian.

"Fine then." She clicks her wallet shut and hurls it back in her purse.

"Things will change," says Brian. "Babies grow up."

A little muscle under her left eye twitches and flutters. "Not always," she sneers. "Look at you."

Yes, look at men: Husbands get sympathetically sick the very minute their wives come down with the flu. They don't clean toilets. They can only handle one thing at a time. They punch out at five. Nothing's their fault. They'd rather be golfing. They are dogs in the institution of marriage. Lumbering, dumb. Always getting tangled up in your legs.

"Why do you do that?" Brian complains.

"What?"

"*That.* Half a fight, and you're not happy until it's a whole one."

"Because you push me to it."

"What have I done?"

"Exactly. What have you done? It takes you three months just to get up in the morning." She watches his expression to see what will happen to it. It wavers. A shiver of satisfaction creeps over her scalp. Brian holds his index finger aloft and begins to say something but doesn't. He gives the air between them a broad sweep with the back of his hand. Then he stomps out. Patty leans against the cutlery drawer. Downstairs the baby is still crying. She can't feel sorry. She hasn't slept. It's all the baby's fault.

Patty charges downstairs yet again. She knocks on the door again. When Joe answers, the light behind his head is dazzling. She steps up to him. "Look at these," she says. She shows him the aggravated pinks of her underlids. "You on the other hand have no wrinkles and the whites of your eyes are still white and I think you could sleep through a nuclear attack and still have good dreams." She begins to work the money in her hand into a tight little tube. "Who gets up at night and feeds that baby? I bet two hundred bucks it isn't you." She prods it into the dorky, ornamental pocket halfway up Joe's sleeve. He backs away, startled by the alien feminine touch, so that she has to lean in to complete the delivery. "Understand?" she asks, stepping down her tone a notch trying not to sound like a small-minded bitch. "Yes?" She nods. "No?" She shakes her head.

Joe shoots her a strange sidelong glance. Perhaps he has no idea what she's saying. But then no one's that stupid when money's around. "That's a gift," she says, pointing to his pocket. "Take the baby to a nice hotel for a night. Or two. Give your poor wife a break."

Patty shuts the door and leans against the wall. Brian measures out tea leaves from one of her little plastic bags not because he likes the taste but because something has come in with her, like a front of black weather. Something that needs a placebo, some calming, some combing down.

Patty rubs her finger back and forth over her thumbnail. She starts to cry. He drops the tea ball into the pot and the chain goes slithering in after it. He walks over to her and takes her hands in his big fists. He kisses the ends of her fingers. He kisses her wet face.

"I hate everything," she says.

"No, you don't," he tells her. She pulls her hands away and presses her fingertips into her eye sockets. The kettle starts to rumble. He collects her in his arms like a tightly bound bundle of something, newspapers or laundry.

She can't see the light in anything. She finds nothing funny. She never did. He wants to feed her a bloody steak in small bites. He wants to lay her out under tropical sun. He wants to carry her into the bedroom and then peel the clothes away. He feels like covering his wife and injecting her with happiness. If only it were transferable, like cash or body heat, this thing that he has that she doesn't. The average contentment she jealously despises, that makes her hate him along with the rest of the world.

Brian arrives in the locker room with his uniform already on and his duffel in hand. He finds the night-shift guys, his old pals, changing from their uniforms into sweatpants and down vests and white sneakers. His supervisor has slotted Brian into daytime detail, a lucky switch, though one made with no explanation. He tries not to think it's because of his new testicular vulnerability.

His locker is marked with his name. He looks at the label, the way in which he formed the letters of his own name so long ago. He opens his locker, and the door falls open with a clang. He drops his bag into the bottom, and when he turns, his buddies have stopped lacing up shoes and fastening Velcro to look at him.

"Hey guys," Brian says tentatively.

"How's it hanging?" they tease, but they've missed him. They slap him on the back and they high-five. They say, "Hey, man, it's good to have you back."

But something's changed or missing or maybe he's just being paranoid. Minutes later they are trickling out of the locker room in a gaggle. He's left there, the first guy to show up for the changing of the guard. Brian sits down on the bench with his jacket on until the day shift arrives, one by one. They mill and unzip. They open and close lockers. How long will it take for them to notice him?

Patty dealt with the neighbours. No more crying. There is so little movement downstairs, Brian begins to forget they all share the house. No longer does he shift limb by limb into bed, apologizing as if Patty has caught him watching porn or kicking the pet they don't have.

They lie on their pillows. "Isn't this nice?" asks Brian.

"Shhh," says Patty. "You'll hex it."

Sleep, after not sleeping, is the most delicious pleasure known to man. They tumble into it and doze through the alarm in the morning. They wake up to the radio show banter of Larry and Willy. They are getting to like it.

It's raining after days with no rain. Pigeons are cooing under the eaves. Patty lifts the elastic of his pajamas. Her light hand settles on his cock and waits there like a thrilling, electric question he's afraid to answer. There's his handicap down there – what if he's lost his aim? But mostly it's been a very long, delicate time between them.

"Does this hurt?" she asks. Her hands probe around. "Does this?"

"You're going to make me late."

"Just answer the question."

"No," he says, "it doesn't hurt at all."

In Yasmin's waiting room, Patty reads a yoga magazine, flipping pages without registering the content. Yasmin comes out to fetch her. Yasmin, with hair drawn back in a slick dark coil, a severe part on the side. She smiles a flat little smile. Patty wonders if she's done something wrong, or if it's just Yasmin's mood. Did someone piss her off? Patty wonders what Yasmin's house looks like and who shares it with her. She wonders if Yasmin is a lesbian.

Patty follows Yasmin into her office and then they begin the procedure. "Lie down," says Yasmin, though Patty knows exactly what to do – this Thursday as with every Thursday. She sits up on the table, then lies back. Yasmin goes to the head of the table and leans over Patty, rubbing her palms together. She plunges her thumbs and fingers into Patty's hair.

Patty tells Yasmin what's gone wrong with her body during the week. Yasmin listens and massages little circles into Patty's scalp. Patty relates the intricacies of her dietary regimens. Yasmin listens and hums. The humming annoys Patty. She begins to embellish the story of her body while reclined on the vinyl, just to see if Yasmin is listening. "I had an all-over rash," Patty says. "I've been experiencing nausea." But none of that is true. Patty has been feeling like an ox, like the healthiest ox on earth.

"Are you hydrated?" Yasmin asks. "Maybe you need a new water filter. Have you thought about buying distilled?"

Yasmin works the base of Patty's skull. "You're loose back there," says Yasmin. "That's good. Most people are very tight."

But Patty doesn't want to be loose or easy. She'd rather be hard, a puzzle for someone to solve. She opens her eyes and peers up at Yasmin. Yasmin stops kneading. She smiles. Upside-down it looks as if she's baring her teeth.

Brian arrives home from work to the aroma of basted meat. He salivates wildly. "What's on?" he says, clutching Patty by the hips.

"Free-range lemon chicken. Roasted tarragon potatoes."

He could kiss the ground, they're eating *food* again, but he doesn't want to discourage her with too much enthusiasm. "I could eat my left arm." He bends to her lips then straightens. "Oh," he says. "You cut your hair." He runs his fingers through a few stubby strands of it.

"Do you like it?" she asks.

"I like it," he says wistfully. "I love it."

When they sit down at the table, Brian devours half his meal without taking his eyes off the plate. Patty falls quiet, knifing little slivers from her vegetables. He's picking chicken flesh from a bone by the time he notices. "What's wrong?" he asks. "Not hungry?" She sets down her knife and her fork on the edge of her plate. She shakes her head. He wonders if she's going to cry.

The phone rings. Patty rushes for it. "Leave it," he says. She sinks back down and dabs at her mouth with her napkin, which she then shoves under the table onto her lap.

The answering machine in the hall whirs and beeps. They listen to a glottal voice. It sounds like no one they know. Somebody overweight. Somebody pissed off. "This is Gus. Remember me? I used to work the day shift. Well listen, pal, I hope you're satisfied. Because now I'm stuck with your shitty night-shift leftovers. What were you thinking, you stupid jerk? You and your busted ball."

Now it's her idea to make love in the middle of the night, though furtively, with the lights out, once she's assured herself that everyone else is asleep. She wants to make up for something. She wants to knock herself out. Brian is going to let her.

He is going to lie on top of her and try to be light. He is going to try not to think of his busted ball. He's going to try and be a good lover. To look down at her and see her as beautiful. He is going to try to be *present* as she's asked – whatever that means. But there's something that keeps distracting him. They are not what they used to be. They are trying too hard.

Downstairs, there is the click of a light switch. It's the start of something. Trouble, or rather, a restlessness. They hear Karam's voice, then Joe's. Lately they've been hearing a lot of midnight conversation: There is an exchange of information. Sometimes the conversation ends in a verbal skirmish and sometimes it just ends. Then there's the aftermath, the flushing of the toilet, the whoosh of water in the pipes. The TV.

Patty whispers, "Stop."

He does, still inside her. He waits. Then thrusts himself deeper as if she won't notice.

"Don't," she says testily. She turns her head on the pillow, straining towards the muffled volley of words. "Now I can't." She slides out from under him, drapes her arm across her forehead as if to cover a fever or a migraine.

"You don't really want to do this, do you?" says Brian.

She closes her eyes and winces. "I spent four thousand dollars at the naturopath."

He props himself up on an elbow. "Say that again."

"Things got a little carried away."

"What things?"

"We're overdrawn." She pummels the pillow and throws herself down on it with a dissatisfied groan. "The MasterCard is in maxed." Brian gapes at the back of her head, his body tingling, his penis at attention.

Cars glide up and down the alley with music streaming from the windows. Kids tear by with balls and sticks and rollerblades. An evening on the cusp of summer. The whole neighbourhood is out in the balm of it.

Brian sips from a wineglass. Patty sits on a lawn chair, arms folded, one knob of bony knee slung over the other. He sets the glass down on the barbecue's wooden slats. He prods and flips things on the grill. Fat drips and flares. When Patty thinks he's not looking, she picks up his glass. He sees her from the corner of his eye. She tips the glass back and a quarter of its contents disappear into her mouth. She puts the glass back, sluices the mouthful around, then swallows. It's an evening on the cusp of everything.

Downstairs there is the opening of a door followed by the bang of the knob on the wall. Patty swivels towards the noise. Brian leans out over the railing. Karam comes into view in an ankle-length bathrobe. She's barefoot. Her hair is undone from its usual tight braid. It fans out down her back, in bobbing, unbrushed waves.

Brian and Patty watch her travel down the driveway. Towards the bottom she steps on something sharp, a piece of gravel or a cube of tempered glass. She lets out a startled yelp and continues into the lane at a limping half-jog. They watch her pink soles flash away in the dusk. As she slips from view behind a garage, they glimpse the hem of her robe, the trailing end of her long skein of hair.

Brian raises his eyebrows at Patty.

"Don't look at me," she says.

Karam reappears on the other side of the garage having picked up some flapping, uncontrolled speed on the laneway's decline. She runs, not to fetch something, but *away* from something. Like a cloud of bees or a tormenting itch. Or out of her own skin. Then she's gone. Slipped out of view behind a cedar hedge.

Joe emerges, walks his measured, stooped walk to the end of the driveway. He stops in the alley, looks right and then left. He glances back at the house and catches sight of Brian and Patty on their balcony. He flashes them a distracted, phony, wobbling smile. Patty lifts her arm into a column of charcoal smoke as if to wave or to beckon. She points after his wife, down to the right, toward the park. Joe doesn't nod or acknowledge the signal. He takes off at a jog with his head down. He doesn't call her name. No one calls her name.

"Should we help or something?"

"Like what did you have in mind?" asks Brian. Call the cops? Phone an ambulance? Weird, private things go on between couples.

Patty steps inside to the kitchen and comes back out with a glass of her own, which she presents to Brian, an empty vessel to be filled. He peers right into the black hole of her pupil while slopping Chardonnay into her glass. They exchange a conversation of looks:

Drinking?

Don't hassle me.

It's been a long time.

I don't care.

Brian holds the tongs aloft. He wears Patty's apron with the geese on it and an oven mitt with geese on it, and suddenly he feels like an ass, like a pussywhipped jerk. He loves his wife madly, unequivocally, madly enough to do whatever the hell she asks. Anything. ANYTHING. He'd kill someone for her, he loves her that much. But right now? Right now he'd love to toss his wine in her face. He'd love to gun her down with an icy spray from the garden hose.

Downstairs a drawer rolls open, and it's a clue. The contents scuttle and collide with the front of the drawer, and someone – Joe, Brian guesses from the roughness of manner – roots around in search of the necessary item. Here's what Brian doesn't hear: Bickering. Snoring. The tapping of toothbrushes against the porcelain in the sink. The stacking of plates in the dish rack. Common, everyday sounds, so boring you don't even pay attention. Downstairs, they sleep in the day and stay up all night. They've been flipped like cushions in a ransacked house.

Where is the baby? Brian and Patty aren't sure, but they have unmentionable ideas. They skulk about in separate bubbles of solitude.

Brian sits down to loosen his laces in the kitchen, making a study of the shoe itself. The grommets, the lace tips, the side-slipped tongue. There's the tick of the clock in the kitchen and the burbling of the drain upstairs. When the shower stops he thinks he can hear Patty drying herself. After a while he lumbers up the stairs, one foot then the next.

He finds her perched on a corner of the bed. Slippers on her feet, legs crossed, hair turbaned in a towel. She pinches the bathrobe closed at her clavicle, rubs the terry between thumb and forefinger. She has lavender puffs under her eyes. There is a plate on the bed. She begins slicing a pear into four. All Brian can see is juice dripping off the blade of her knife. She wraps the pear wedge in prosciutto. She folds it into her mouth. What business does she have eating food like that? "Where the hell did you get that ham?" Brian demands. "How much did it cost?"

What are babies but a fraction of an adult? It was one-tenth the size of Patty. One-tenth of her weight and adult proportions. An unformed personality. A sickly, soft-boned, toothless creature. Perhaps a tenth is too much. How about half of a tenth? A twentieth. A fraction of a fraction.

Do they go down? Do they ask? How will they know for sure?

Babies are the commonest, easiest thing to make. Everywhere, all over the world, people wind up with little reproductions of themselves. Mothers jerk them around in the bath trying to lather soap onto all the right body parts, trying to wash the dirt of life from their faces and armpits. They shake the poop out of diapers. But it's no use. You can't make life fair just by getting it clean.

Anxiety sits like a brown clayey lump in the middle of her mind. Patty can't push it around. Why worry? It's a useless emotion. It's not real. It can't touch her. She decides to march forth in her thoughts. The car is nice. She is going to be happy and positive. She's going to sit in deep traffic, listening to a dreamy male voice on the radio. She's going to imagine what this man looks like, and if he would find her sexy.

Then, while she's stopped at the intersection, there's an ambulance. Its lights flash in her rear-view. There are too many cars. It's a tight situation. She's stopped too close to the minivan in front of her. She honks at the driver to move up. He glances at her in his mirror and then back to the car in front of him. Behind her, the streams of traffic are parting. The ambulance is upon her, its siren insisting in its professional way that she move, move, move. She cranks the wheel and clenches her teeth, breathing, breathing deeply all the time. The car is her enclave of warmth and protection. She wedges it out of her lane between the minivan and a pickup parked at the curb. The ambulance proceeds, as it must. It squeaks by her door, a big white box. As it passes, the paramedic in the passenger seat shoots her a nasty look. *Get the hell out of the way.* The paramedic with his fleece vest and his short white sleeves. Why? It's not her fault she's involved. Nothing is her fault.

The ambulance speeds away, but somehow not fast enough. What about the person on the gurney in the back? Is she dying? Is someone holding her hand? The mere thought of it makes the tears crest on the rims of her eyelids. But now she's waited too long to get back into the flow on the street. Now she's waiting some more, nosing into the stream of cars whose owners pretend not to see her. Her neck hurts from craning. She butts back in. A car honks and she's clouded in a sudden fog of emotion. When the time comes, who will want to hold Patty's hand? Her life is too small, her desires too selfish and nasty. Who will sit by her hospital bed while tubes pump fluids to replenish what has leaked? She feels like she's leaking right now. Who will applaud when she triumphs over death? She's back in the thick of the rush-hour tide. She lets it carry her home. She turns her corner. It's too close to home to cry.

Three women stand in the driveway, two young, one old. They have noses exactly like every woman Patty has ever seen enter the downstairs apartment. They stare. Patty smiles. They don't. As she climbs the steps, Patty feels their eyes on the triangle of scarf across her back, her stockinged calves where the muscles begin to burn. She has the key ready in her hand. She scurries inside and closes the door and leans her full weight against it.

Brian slouches in to greet her. He's so slow and dour. He's got something to tell her, she can tell. It's going to be creepy and bad. The light fades in the house. Brian approaches. He tries to wrap his hand around hers. She slaps him away. He wants to slather her with sympathy. He wants to drool all over her parade. Cars and more purring cars in the driveway. Doors thud softly. Clouds slide over the sun – her least favourite weather of all, when you want to turn the lights on before it's even dark. Their apartment is too white. They never entertain. They need to cover the walls. Polite little heels click across the asphalt. Downstairs the apartment fills with murmuring women. What's the matter with these people downstairs? They're not normal. Why don't they shout and kick holes in the walls? Why don't they scream at the ceiling and be done with it? *Go fuck yourselves,* she'd love to yell out over the rooftops. She doesn't want their news. They can keep their goddamn news to themselves. She's going to call up some people and invite them for dinner. She's worked hard for this mood. This unbearably fantastic mood.

HEATHER O'NEILL

The Difference Between
Me and Goldstein

When I was little, we lived in West Virginia. A lot of people wouldn't talk to us, because my family had a bad reputation. My mother had a tattoo of a butterfly on her wrist that fit under her watch when she was going to my uncle's parole hearing. She put mascara on and her hair up, but you could always tell right off the bat that she was wild.

My mother met my father when she ran away from home to the city in 1969. He was a guru. He would just sit in the park philosophizing with young people sitting around him. My mother wrote down what he said in a notebook. She thought it was like being educated. My dad always scared women because he had a nail for a front tooth and was crazy about shot guns. My mother was nineteen and had long hair down to her butt and she was crazy about him. My mother used to wake us up in the middle of the night when she was drinking. She would drag us out into the yard to look at the full moon. My mother was the kind of woman who calls you in the middle of the night begging you for forty dollars so that she can leave town or else she'll be murdered. There was always a pile of clothes and broken chairs in the yard in the front of our house. There was pot growing in the pigpen and the goats walked around the house. Now I live in the city.

"My friends are all afraid of you!" Goldstein says. "How come you didn't make a single friend from college?"

Goldstein has lots of friends. He goes and meets them for coffee. Growing up, we were never allowed to use the term "best friend" in my house. My dad said a best friend is someone who will rat you out in the future. "Your family are your only friends."

Goldstein was born in Brooklyn. He likes comic books, Chris Elliot, and National Lampoon. If someone leaves their hat on a seat on the subway, he feels terrible. He likes radio documentaries about transvestites and eccentric babysitters. He opens the window of the bus when we pass by the chocolate factory. You can imagine him reading *Charlie and the Chocolate Factory* as a child.

He's a vegetarian and he likes Thai food. He smokes cigarettes and doesn't inhale. He blows out all the smoke with his lips pursed and smiles. He compliments an old woman on the flowers that she planted in her one-foot city garden. He is terrified of rats. He didn't have any girlfriends in high school and he used to sit in peep shows between classes in university. He finds the girls from 1920s silent films pretty. He likes to write haikus in black notebooks at the doctor's office. He likes to play MS PAC-MAN and drink Orangina.

He likes to sit for tea squeezed between old Chinese men on a bench in a cafeteria in Chinatown. He likes to stand on a bridge that goes over a polluted river and calls it our romantic spot. He gets us to both stand on the fortune-telling scale. He is delighted when the paper comes out saying 270 lbs; "Your future is bright." He says he will keep it and tell people that he has come a long way.

He says he doesn't like when I act tough. I pick flowers and stick them behind my ear and give people the evil eye. I like horses that have got lost. I especially love crazy roosters. I like the idea of black sheep. I like people who think they're lucky when they're not. I like people with long long legs that look like they belong on a motorcycle. I like blue eyes you can see across the room. The lights of motels on the highway make me feel like I'm in love with everyone, even the people on death row. I like busted-up cars with stuffed animals all over the seats and stickers on the hood. I like scrap men with thick dirty arms in pickups filled with old stoves. I like bare feet sticking out of car windows. I like Hells Angels when fifty of them pass down the highway at once. I like when a train passes right next to me. I like people who come up to your door trying to sell you stolen quilts. I like the pickpockets at the bus depot who pretend to be in love with you. I like birds and tattoos of birds.

I doodle stars all over my notebook until the paper looks like a night sky when you are lying on a pillow in the grass. Goldstein and I are trying to figure out where to settle down together. I want to buy a farm. Not the kind where you necessarily grow anything. The kind where you can stand in the yard in your underwear, where you can talk to yourself and nobody knows any different. Where you can have chickens named Peeper and Frederick. Goldstein doodles rockets and mad scientists. He doodles an open window through which you can see an attractive fat woman watching television. He says if he could buy any car he says he'd buy a little Honda because it's easy to park. Goldstein carries around a tape recorder and records people performing music on the street. He plays the tape back to me. It's of two punks making up a song.

"This made me think of you," he says.

He says he has a beautiful picture in his head of us sitting outside the New York Public Library eating peanut butter sandwiches.

TIM MITCHELL

Night Finds Us

Here's a hollow thump when it hits the wall again, no more fat or bone in its body than in a baby's fist. It slips back toward the carpet, wings tapping the wall on the way down. Under the covers, I try to turn myself to stone, not even moving my chest when I breathe. Eventually though, without taking my eyes away from the wall, I risk edging a hand toward Julia. I poke her side, aiming for her ribs, but actually pushing into one of her breasts.

"Quit it," she whispers, still asleep.

I lean closer. "There's a bat in the room."

The words sink into her. Julia doesn't say anything, but draws in a breath and holds it long inside her. She opens those eyes, healthy eyes that don't need glasses, don't need to be cleared with knuckles to see in the dark. Julia looks straight at the ceiling, not searching the room or the air at all. I think, *She doesn't believe me.*

Then, in one fast motion, Julia rolls onto her side, pushes my shoulders into the mattress, and clamps her hand over my mouth. Panicked, I drag breath in through my nose, but she kisses me, light on the bridge of my nose. Her hand floats away like a seed. It is her oldest cure, and it works again: I wake up.

My body is clenched in shock, but relaxes at the stillness of the room. There is no bat.

"Sorry," I say, embarrassed to have done this again.

Julia pats my cheek: *not to worry*.

I glance around the room, trying to remember what's real and what isn't. "It's the same night?" I ask.

Julia nods in the dark. She says softly, "Yeah."

There's a pause as we both give each other the chance to say more, then one of us reaches to hold the other, and we become more asleep than awake.

When Julia left me, she left the whole city, driving straight to the Tsawwassen ferry terminal in our worn-out car, its timing belt fraying and its locks chipped with rust. She spent only ten minutes packing and accidentally left behind her toothbrush and all her rolls of film. She made a point of taking her foil ashtrays, though. She walked through the apartment finding each one, placing them with a *click* into her coat pocket. They were the last thing we'd argued about.

Long before we moved into this apartment, Julia told me that she didn't believe in true love. She believed that a person could be happy with any one of a number of other people in the world. I was already in love with her then and felt as though I should argue, but of course she's probably right. When we met, she had just ended a three-year relationship with a man named Jim, the manager of a children's theatre on Vancouver Island, where she used to live. "In a way, I'll always love him too," she said once.

I nodded, not sure how to answer. "Of course you will."

Two weeks after Julia left, her mail stopped arriving at the apartment. I packed cardboard boxes full of everything she'd left behind and waited for her to write for them. After a month, I drew up a list of women's shelters on blue-lined paper and taped it to the bottom box. That night, I dreamt that silverfish ate the list, ate the cardboard, ate the photo-negatives of her friends. I woke up kneeling on the boxes, trying to scare away the creatures with a flashlight that wasn't turned on.

Julia came back tonight, after two months and twenty days. I never did send the boxes away.

She stood over our bed, trying to decide whether I was awake or not, her eyes still unused to the dark. She was wearing a thick wool sweater, wool socks, wool gloves – her winter coat was folded in a box. It must have been raining outside, because in the faint reflected light from the hall, I could see water caught in the wool.

"Before we decide anything," she said, "you should know that I'm pregnant." There was a strange note of sympathy in her voice, as though I'd been hurt and didn't know. Rather than ask, I pulled back the covers. Stepping out of all that wool, her skin was hot.

For the third time tonight, I wake up in the dark. It's 4 a.m. and Julia isn't here. I'm not ready for this, and my body feels jarred as though I've miscounted stairs in the dark.

But then I hear the fridge close in the kitchen and see her woollen clothes on the floor. I am sick of not being able to tell dreams from the real world. I switch on a light, dig out my slippers, and force myself to stop studying the carpet as though expecting to see droppings or tufts of fur.

My mother had dreams as intense as mine, as did her father, and grandfather, and other parents so dead that no one remembers them. Mostly, my mother dreamt about storms. She would barricade our windows with pillows or spread her hands across the panes to feel the force of a rain that wasn't there. When I was two years old, my mother carried my baby sister into our basement pantry and sat without a light or blanket on the concrete floor, beside shelves full of jellies and dark, stewed plums. My father eventually found the two of them, but my mother refused to be led back to bed. She couldn't understand why my father hadn't brought me down to shelter as well. "Tell me," she insisted, pulling against my father's hand. "Tell me, goddammit. He's dead, isn't he?"

My father, exhausted, finally said, "All right, he's dead." Years later, when he left, my father gave us a number of reasons, but he never mentioned the dreams.

It's chilly in the bedroom tonight, so before going to check on Julia in the kitchen, I pull out a turtleneck, decide it's not enough, and hunt for a sweater. On the dresser top, I notice a Wal-Mart receipt with Jim's phone number on it in my handwriting. I wonder for a moment if Julia has seen it or not. Jim phoned from his home on the island a week after Julia left to tell me she was staying there.

"Julia didn't want me to tell you," he said, "and I would appreciate it if you didn't call, but I wanted you to know she was safe. We are all adults, after all." But I'm twenty-six and he's thirty-five, so I didn't know whether he meant this or not.

I never used the phone number, telling myself that calling Julia would be an invasion. Nonetheless, I don't want her to know that I had the chance. I throw the paper out in the pail by my dresser, rearranging the garbage so that envelopes and Tim Hortons cups are on top.

Suddenly exasperated with myself, I straighten up, scratch at my hair, and look around the room. There's no reason left for me to stay in here.

The only light on is the one above the stove. Julia sits near it, eating a slice of toast off our cutting board. She's mixed together strawberry jam and peanut butter on the same piece of bread.

"I didn't mean to wake you up," she says.

"I should be saying that to you." I cross my thumbs and mime a bat with my hands. She smiles, and when I kiss her, she tries to keep toast crumbs from falling on me.

"Not your fault," she says.

We are both being as carefully kind to each other as a couple just starting out. Perhaps there really is that little left between us; it scares me that I don't know.

Julia and I smile at each other while she eats. There isn't any other bread left, so I put a hot dog bun in the toaster, and then occupy myself with positioning the buns properly and knotting the bag. It's not until Julia finishes her toast and stands with the empty cutting board in front of her that we are finally forced to say something.

"You have Jim's number on your dresser," she says.

I want to know if she was happy there. I want to know if she is back for good. I want to know if she understands that I'm sorry.

"Why did you leave him?" I ask.

Julia's eyes seem to wander over my sweater. "Are you going to want me to have this baby tested?" she asks.

It's a huge question, but I ignore it, because I know the answer she wants. "No," I say. "Why would I? Of course not."

She's quiet for a moment and unplugs the toaster without thinking about it. Its glow stops. She says, "We really should be asleep."

Nothing is happening, but nonetheless, I know it's a dream. Outside, the streets are wet; cars make a tearing sound in the water as they pass. It's intermittent enough to be lonely.

There's a scamper of movement by the radiator. Something scuffs over the carpet, hangs on the outside of the radiator, pulls itself in through the bars. Shadowed, it sits in what it thinks is secrecy, but it has forgotten its tail, which hangs down out of the radiator, thin and furred. One and then two monkeylike fingers curl around the bars.

Julia's arm is across me. She's asleep. This time, I don't wake her up, because I am so sure that none of this is real. I try to force this knowledge onto myself, but the creature stays there, its tail whisking the carpet, its breath patient. Water runs into the corner of my mouth. I may know this is a nightmare, but my body is crying from fear all the same.

I give up trying to wake up. For the moment, I believe that these nightmares have nothing to do with genes, but come from some ancestor of mine who turned away the wrong stranger. I cannot imagine not having Julia here to hold when I wake up. And this thought alone brings me across into the waking world. The radiator is empty.

Gently as I can, I put my head on her tummy. She draws one long breath again, but doesn't wake up. I lie there, listening to the same sounds that surround this child-to-be. Sleepily, I become convinced that the child will be a boy and he will have Julia's eyes: clear and serious. I pray he will be healthy, I pray he will love us, and I pray that when he sleeps, he will see murderers, his heart pounding against his small ribs as though trapped with something evil. I wonder quietly if this makes me a bad father.

JACQUELINE HONNET

Conversion Classes

Your mother calls to say your cousin's husband is becoming Catholic. You cradle the receiver against your shoulder and rearrange the condiments in your fridge door. Your cousin had no idea he was taking conversion classes, she says, Can you imagine that? You toss a sticky mustard container into the garbage and wonder why *your* husband keeps putting balsamic vinegar in the fridge. You assure your mother you are listening and repeat the words: Sacraments of Initiation at St. Cecilia's, Easter Sunday. You pull the cap off the dry-erase pen with your teeth, write SECOND COMING AT ST. CECILIA'S, EASTER on the white board beside the phone and agree this is a blessing.

Your husband was baptized, but no longer goes to mass – except for Christmas, which he likes, and Good Friday, which he doesn't. The endless kneeling, he laughs. Up and down and up and down, it's enough to make you pass out. You have fainted twice, both times on Good Friday during the reading of the Passion. When Father Julian gets to the part where they cut Jesus' side, and then the water and the blood and the sharp cabbage breath of the woman beside you with the lazy eye, the too-high singing voice. A kaleidoscope of light swirls before you, which would be a comfort if you could focus, lift your heavy hands. You awake in the foyer, staring at Sister Stephanie's thin wooden cross swinging toward you until she clutches it to her chest. She strokes your hot face with a thin cool hand, A powerful day, isn't it, dear? Your husband kneels beside you, his hand on his own forehead, unaware he yanked your dress above your waist as he carried you behind the pews and out the chapel door. Your faded blue polka-dot silk panties are visible, the ones you told him to wash by hand and he forgot, put them in the washer anyway.

You are wearing the same panties the day you find your wedding dress. In a store called Precious. The sort of place that promises class, then asks you to remove your shoes and check large purses at the counter. Your mother crouches in the store entrance and pulls off her brown loafers, says, Let's separate and meet in twenty minutes – trust me, I'm an expert. You smile at her over a display of pearl-studded veils and headpieces adorned with silk flowers, as she hoists an off-the-shoulder gown triumphantly and mouths: Success. You think, a smarter woman wouldn't have brought her mother wedding dress shopping. That woman is by herself in a vintage dress shop, trusting her own instincts. That woman is slipping into a simple empire-waist gown, smiling at her reflection in the large three-way mirror of her private change room.

You picture this woman as you stand in the communal dressing room lined with padded benches and sheets of mirror, beside a large woman with a shiny face and wispy brown hair whose mother cries each time she tries on a dress. She dabs a tissue into the corner of each perfectly lined eye. Honey, suck in your stomach. Stand on your tiptoes. Don't rest your arms on your sides – remember arm fat. Gasp. Tissue please. Your mother glances at that mother, hands you a princess-waist dress and rolls her eyes. This dress has pearl beading around the neck and your mother says, Honey, it's subtle, just try it. She clutches her hands to her chest. Is that not perfect? It is so perfect. Excuse me for intruding, the crying mother says, I love it too. Is that your daughter? She's so beautiful. A tissue?

You take this as an omen. Your mother never cries and you never wear white. You swore you'd pick a cream dress, one that didn't reach the floor and had no beads. You had friends with dresses so ornate that on their wedding days they were hard to hug. They moved in a blur of teeth and pearls, touching shoulders and whispering, Thank you. You smile at your mother in the mirror – convinced she's hoping you'll look the same way.

Do we have to go to the baptism?
Yes.
Can we –
Can we what? – Can we just call instead? Can *I* just go alone with my mother?
Calm down.
We will not be one of *those* couples.
What couples?
The ones where the wives show up to everything and say, *Oh, Bob was feeling a bit under the weather.*
My throat *does* feel a bit sore.
Come here.
Ouch.

You are looking through the glovebox for a piece of gum when you tell your husband you want to go to New Orleans for Mardi Gras. Like that documentary where women flashed their boobs at the Mardi Gras parade for strings of beads? he asks. You only lasted five minutes on our honeymoon without a bikini top. – Am

I burning? Are my nipples burning? Do you see anyone we know? Doesn't *he* look like our dry cleaner at home, except with hair? It's your second day in Bora Bora and a woman from New York with breasts as big as watermelons lies topless by the pool. Marketing, she tells the man beside her as she lathers her left breast with suntan lotion. – I make brochures, Web sites, billboard ads, that sort of thing. You peer over the top of your sunglasses and try to picture her in a business suit, each of her breasts straining against the thin rayon of her corporate blouse. Mama, your husband says enthusiastically in your ear. The woman's breasts glow hot and pink by late afternoon and you say, That's what happens when you're exposed for too long. You pretend to read your magazine and watch with envy the French and Italian mothers with babies and bellies and oversized sunglasses as they oil their sturdy, dark breasts. Your husband claims he likes your pale, tender ones best.

Celeste, the hostess in the main dining room, has lemon-coloured hair, which reaches the middle of her back; she flips pieces over her shoulders as she tells your husband he has lovely blue eyes. You teasingly call her his girlfriend. But before supper you spend an hour getting dressed, tying and retying your sarong according to the colourful diagram on the small square of gift shop cardboard. The sarongs in the picture make those women look sexy like Celeste, not gift-wrapped like you. You pour yourself another glass of white wine and adjust the material in front of the mirror. Your husband slips off the bed and rubs your shoulders. When you lived in your own apartment you got dressed alone, tossing belts and scarves in a frustrated heap. There was no one to comment. Your cheeks flush and you want to push him away. Instead, you ask him to hang up the thick terry cloth bathrobe that sits at your feet, the one he presented to you unceremoniously on your wedding night. You bought him a wallet. You both agree practical presents are best, so why can't you stop thinking about the silver hoop earrings you really wanted the birthday he bought you an AMA membership saying, I'll renew it every year, okay?

You clean out your spare bedroom. You usually keep this door closed and when you open it, a pleasing burst of cool air blasts your face. You kneel in front of the closet with your clear blue recycling bag and pull pant legs and skirt hems until they form a pile. You pretend you are getting ready for an extended house-guest and, therefore, must be ruthless. You have so much in storage: a second (and third) wok, a clear plastic shower curtain embossed with goldfish (it matched the orange shag carpet in your first apartment), boxes of mugs with pictures of hummingbirds (they match an incomplete set of dishes you left in your parents' basement). You have already given much away. But one more box will make you feel freer. You have a friend whose downtown apartment contains only a denim-covered loveseat, a metal barstool, a blue air mattress, and a silver gooseneck lamp. Total freedom, she says. She has a better job than you, but seldom buys anything. You shop with her once when she's replacing her black dress pants. All I need is one pair, she says walking out of the change room. How else could I afford so many Mexico trips? You admire her vigilance and try to banish sentimentality as you look for something, anything to stuff into the blue bag and mark with an X for the Community Living Foundation that calls for monthly donations of gently used clothes and small household items. You remind yourself that last month you gave away a black jacket you liked, and then spent an hour the following Saturday digging through racks of pink trench coats and maternity capes at Value Village hoping to find that jacket on the $10 or less rack. This time you promise your husband you won't get "desperate to donate"; you'll choose more carefully. You throw in clothes of his you've always hated. The brown sweatshirt that makes him look round and the faded blue jeans that are too high in the waist. How can he miss them if he doesn't even know they're gone?

You find your wedding dress in the closet. Not *find* really, you knew it was there all along. You discover it the way people discover the courage to clip fingernails on new babies or say the word *forever*. Feel the fear and do it anyway, you read somewhere, and wonder why things that are easy to say are never easy to do. You slip out of your jeans and take your wedding dress off its pink quilted hanger. Pull it over your black socks and blue cotton panties, twist your arm behind your back and hold your breath as you pull the tiny zipper. It moves smoother than you expect, and you are surprised at how good you look. That it fits. You sigh laboriously. Everything about you is so different now, from the colour of your hair (French Roast Brown) to the way you give certain advice (ask for a refund – it shouldn't be unraveling). How could your body be exactly the same? You remember that you forgot to have the dress dry cleaned right after the wedding, like you were supposed to. It was hot that day and the church had no air conditioning. The lilies drooped and you sweated, but the armpits of the dress are not yellowed, as you'd expect. You press the smooth fabric to your nose and are comforted that one year later the delicate scent of Escape lingers. You take the dress off quickly when the car lights flood the bedroom window. You don't want to hear your husband say he still loves the way the dress exposes your collarbone, and those small nodules at the base of your neck where your hair rests. You'd rather hear him say that the dress doesn't suit you any more – that it's too confining. You want to hear him say that you'd be a different bride now. Just a simple cream sheath dress, loose hair, open-toed sandals.

∾

Would you have converted for me?

I *am* Catholic.

A lapsed Catholic – you aren't even confirmed.

You, Ms. Catholic, didn't even want to go to the marriage prep.
    classes.

That's different.

How?

I just thought they'd be different. – I just thought it would all be
    different.

Waiting for your first marriage preparation course, you sit
holding your future husband's hand on the host couple's dark
brown couch, its armrest doilies crisply starched with scalloped
edges. Trays of mini sausage rolls, Nanaimo bars, and butter
cookies cover the small coffee table. You rub your foot over the
criss-cross pattern left by the vacuum and watch the host wife
pour tea from a white ceramic pot into delicate teacups – different months of the year written in script on each saucer. The
host husband keeps readjusting himself in his chair. You smile
politely and compliment their immaculate home. Three words
for you honey, the host wife says – hire a maid. You laugh nerv-
ously as she carefully hands you a teacup. Your saucer says
October (your mother's birthday) and your future husband's
says May (yours), and you'd ask him to trade if you didn't think
it would seem strange. I got spring, your future husband says,
and you got Halloween – spooky. The host wife starts the
evening with the Lord's prayer, and you motion to your future
husband to cross himself. She informs you both, smiling, that
she and the host husband were separated for six months two
years ago, and they feel the experience better prepared them to
counsel couples awaiting marriage. You think *awaiting* is a
strange word to use, as though you are not frenzied, meeting
with the caterer who says she won't serve just fish, or attending

a third dress fitting where the seamstress assures you you *will* be able to breathe once the bodice seams are loosened.

By week four you are discussing *The Power of Expectation and Assumption*. You read, *The questions on the back of this page are meant to identify our assumptions. But remember, as we are free to keep our present expectations, we are also free to make changes to our ways of thinking to ensure a happier partnership.* You and your future husband sit alone at the host couple's kitchen table, eating mini bagel pizzas, drinking raspberry tea, and completing your worksheets. *This tendency to presume that others see things our way is called projection*, he reads aloud. You smile at him, take another sip of raspberry tea.

(1) I think I should be able to spend____dollars without consulting my spouse after we marry. You write $300 confidently, but then claim the three is in fact a messy one when your future husband says $50. *(2) When do I think our first child will be born?* You skip this question. *(3) My assumption about weekend worship is that we will_____.* And this one too. Later in the car, you tell your future husband that you can discuss these questions when you've both had more time to think.

You have supper at your favourite Vietnamese restaurant one month before your wedding. As your future husband hangs both your jackets on the wooden coat rack, you see the host wife in a booth with a man. You recognize the back of her head, her tight coppery curls. You catch her reflection in the mirrors that line the restaurant walls and see her face. The way her body curves toward this man. The way she touches her neck every time she speaks. You sit across the restaurant. Your eyes meet momentarily and you look away. You dip your salad roll into fish sauce and tell yourself she'll come over and introduce the man as her co-worker. She doesn't.

You decide to send your cousin's husband an online card, but can't find one appropriate for the occasion. Happy Conversion? Happy Transformation? Happy Metamorphosis? Happy Rebirth? Happy Sanctification? Congratulations on your upcoming baptism and confirmation.

You are sitting on the futon in the basement – your bed until you could afford a real one – not watching the TV flickering in the corner, and explaining to your husband why you want to drive to Vancouver alone to visit an old friend. Couples do this all the time, you say, take separate vacations. He shakes his head and says, How can you drive to Vancouver alone when you have trouble unlocking the gas cap on the car? I worked with a woman who drove her Jeep Wagoneer to Whitehorse alone and *her* boyfriend called her adventurous and brave, you say. Someone driving to Vancouver with an AMA membership and a cellphone is neither. Someone like *that* can drive anywhere she wants. You can still smell the butter on the popcorn kernels as you collect the bowls and bottles from the table and walk upstairs. Your husband shouts, Why are you referring to yourself in the third person? This is the same way you told him you were quitting your job. If, for instance, *someone* is unfulfilled in her career and has a clear sense of what she wants to do, she should do it – of course taking her spouse into consideration.

You load the dishwasher – rearrange bowls, rinse chunks of lettuce off dinner dishes he loaded earlier, and remove the Tefal pots that he's already ruined. He makes you a cup of green jasmine tea and sets up the Scrabble board on the kitchen island. You dry your hands on a tea towel and quickly spell OX off the

end of his PHOENIX. He claims you are too impetuous, not com-
mitted enough, and it's why you seldom win. You remember
your mother on Sundays in the kitchen as you played Trivial
Pursuit with your father in the next room. You tugged on her
pants and said, Please, please come sit down, but settled for
putting a brown teddy bear in her place. She never sat down, and
now you imagine she's probably like you and prefers the warm,
lemon-scented privacy of doing dishes.

I'm becoming my mother.
Does that mean I'm becoming your father or my father?
Seriously, I'm answering these marriage prep. questions like my
    mother would.
Like what?
What component is <u>*most*</u> *essential to a good marriage: friend-
    ship, intimacy, trust, or passion?*
Intimacy. No, passion.
Friendship – I said friendship, my mother would say friendship.
You *are* my very best friend.
Shut up.
See – passion.

You are on your way out the door when your mother calls. You
stand on the doormat sorting through bills and answer, No, to
all of her questions. Do you know what you are wearing to the
baptism? Do you want to go shopping then? Do you want to
borrow my mauve dress? You know, the silk one with the pearl
buttons. Are you just being difficult? You'll want to look your
best, she says, I'll drop off my mauve dress.

Before you meet a friend for coffee, you spend fifteen minutes putting your hair in pigtails, the kind that sit low on your head and make you look trendy and young. You wear the silver hibiscus-shaped earrings your mother gave you as a teenager, the ones that used to jingle whenever you moved your head. You snipped the extra dangling pieces off with wire cutters. Your husband called you crazy for ruining perfectly good earrings, but sat beside you on the bathroom counter and rasped the exposed edges smooth. You meet your friend in a tiny café with old velvet couches, thin woollen rugs, and the smell of cedar incense and burnt coffee. You choose a deep red chair and sink below the arm rests, hoping the guy on the barstool with the sideburns and the thumb ring is smiling at you and not your pigtails. Your girlfriend plunks herself down and says, You look precious with those piggy tails, as she fiddles with your left earring. You smile and ask yourself why you don't call her more often. You're on your second sip of coffee when she says, I'm living with a bush pilot, we met six weeks ago. He's perfect, he plays in a jazz band, has two Dobermans, and cut my first initial into his chest with an X-Acto knife the night we met. Three cups of coffee later, she adds nonchalantly that her boyfriend looks exactly like your husband. You walk down the street outside the café and she is holding your hand as you try to picture your husband as a bush pilot instead of a civil engineer, as someone dangerous. You ask her, Is it like they could be brothers, or only distant cousins? Even in your platform sandals you are slightly shorter. She grabs your shoulders, kisses your forehead enthusiastically, and says, You are so funny, married lady – I just love you. Out of sight, you stop and look at yourself in the window of a used bookstore, pull the ponytails out of your hair, and shake your head violently from side to side. By the time you reach your car your hands are shaking from the coffee and you remind yourself that even one cup makes you edgy.

Do I seem different?

Different how?

Do I still seem fun and adventurous – like someone you'd call about a rave or where to buy pot?

But you don't smoke pot.

Just answer the question.

No, you don't seem like that.

No, I *don't* seem fun and adventurous?

No, the pot thing – God, you've never even smoked a cigarette.

I could have.

After two bottles of red wine your husband tells his friend about an expensive dress you only wore once. Too low cut, he laughs, drawing a modest scoop across your throat with his finger. You laugh too. Try it on, his friend says playfully. You bought the chocolate-coloured wraparound dress for your cousin's baby's christening, and when you picked up your mother she said, Ooh sexy. You figured she was being funny, but the sound of the word filled the car and for the rest of the day you pretended to play with your pearl necklace. At the christening, your mother admired the pink baby and your cousin's simple black pantsuit, the way it minimized her swollen chest. Something like *that* would be obscene if you were a lactating mother, she said eyeing your cleavage. You sold the dress that winter in a consignment store, which your husband wouldn't understand, so you take your glass of red wine upstairs and come down in your iridescent green high school graduation dress instead. Strapless, a neckline so low you had to dig your black bustier out of the bottom drawer of your dresser, the drawer which contains the champagne-coloured negligee you forgot to pack for your honeymoon, and the silky thong underwear you purchased before realizing you aren't a thong underwear person. The underwire on the bustier digs into your armpits. Your husband's eyes widen as he gulps his wine, but his friend smiles approvingly.

For months after, your husband asks you to put the green dress on before you have sex. It's like we're dating again, he says. You don't like the way it reminds you of a girl you worked with whose boyfriend convinced her to shave off her pubic hair to spice things up. He said, You feel like someone new. Sometimes you catch her scratching in the ladies room, her hand down the front of her skirt. She says she'll think twice about doing it again. Again? Your husband says, Weird, and wonders if you'd ever do the same. You decide he's being rhetorical, kiss the top of his head, and add more milk to your tea.

You try to look unfettered when the woman tells you about the shaving – sitting in the passenger seat of her new Volkswagen – the way you do when she recounts the night she is drunk and kisses Jill in accounting. She says women's lips are more delicate than men's. She smiles, calls you beautiful, and you are afraid she might kiss you too. You keep this secret from your husband, along with the fact that you forgot to wear your wedding band the weekend you took CPR certification, that you kissed your brother-in-law on the lips by mistake on New Year's Eve.

You are lying on your bed looking at the ceiling as you dial your cousin's number. I heard about the new convert, you say enthusiastically into the phone. He's going to be baptized too, hey? At least he's big enough; you won't need to hold his head over the baptismal font. You fold up the map of Vancouver you had spread across the bed and swing your feet over the side. Tell him that if he changes his mind, fainting doesn't work; the priest will take it as a sign of overwhelming faith. If he's a good little soldier we'll bring him chocolate Easter eggs instead of a rosary. You hang up, stuff the map in your bottom drawer, and wonder if women with babies and newly baptized husbands collect street maps of places they'd like to go.

You are admiring your now sparse storage closet. You climb inside, sit cross-legged on a square of blue carpet, and look up at black garment bags and thin plastic covers that contain clothes you are not ready to give away. But from where you are sitting the closet looks crowded and you wonder if you should reconsider keeping your cream and red sundress, your navy blue skirt, and your black linen pants, their hems resting on your shoulders.

You lie in until noon on Saturday, and decide that if you don't get up you won't feel pressured to go with your mother to the funeral of her neighbour's aunt. She calls Friday, saying, Your father isn't feeling up to it, and besides, us women are better at small talk. In your mind you scream, It's not admirable to only be good at surface conversation. But you say, Maybe, and write TOTAL STRANGER'S FUNERAL below NAIL POLISH REMOVER on your white board.

Downstairs, you hear the clink and sizzle of your husband making coffee and eggs. Your weekend routine – he ate hours ago as he read the *Globe and Mail* and will soon come up with breakfast and tell you about the stories he's read. He fixates on the sad ones involving children being mistreated or even killed, and recounts the events in soft tones, his forehead wrinkled, eyes clear and deliberate. You listen to him as you eat your eggs and ask questions like, where was the baby boy's father? (at work), how cold was it? (-17), and how did they get him off the balcony? (they didn't). He moves the empty serving tray, tosses the paper beside the bed, and slips into the crumb-filled sheets for a quick nap. You have never known another adult who gets tired when he is sad. He is seven when his grandfather dies, his sobbing mother hangs up the phone, piles her four children on top of the plaid comforter of her queen-sized bed in the middle of a hot summer afternoon, and hums "Moon River" until they drift off. He says he always feels better when he wakes up – even if he only sleeps for a few minutes. You yelled at him to stop asking if you wanted to take a nap the morning you packed for your grandmother's funeral, but now you lie beside him, hold his hand, and watch him sleep. A web of blue veins barely perceptible through his pale skin as his chest rises and falls.

You want me to get confirmed then?
No – that's not it.
Then what's the big deal?
I just feel like getting married has changed me more than you.
I've gained more weight.
Is that supposed to make me feel better?
You could start smoking pot – would that make you feel better?
Why won't you take me seriously?

It's Sunday. Conversion day. You are wearing your mother's mauve silk A-line. You study yourself in the full-length mirror and think the A-line makes you look like somebody else; somebody more contented, more accepting, more compliant. You push your hands down the sides of the skirt. Decide the thin fabric will smooth with control-top pantyhose. You walk towards the full-length mirror, you walk away. Rip off the silky folds and grab the green dress with the flared skirt your husband thinks looks like peppermint antacid. You pull it on, stand on your tiptoes. You pirouette. You twirl. Forget the pantyhose. You're ready. You grab the duffel bag you packed last night and head downstairs. One hour and your cousin's husband will take the wafer on his tongue and transform himself into a brand-new person. One hour and you'll be driving west, listening to Alanis Morissette and maybe even smoking a cigarette.

ANNE FLEMING

Gay Dwarves of America

He ran his finger up and down the slight snake of King Street: King Street South, bend, King Street North, slither, King Street West, bend-slither, King Street East. The only main street in the country that went four ways. Back to King Street South. Which was his problem. How to make it work. How to revitalize it. Every idea he had was trite, unoriginal.

He turned his eraser on its side.

– Rmmm-rmmm, he said. He ran the eraser over to Fairview Mall and plowed into its walls.

– Bring out the wrecking ball, he said, stabbing the eraser with the unfolded paper clip he'd been using to pick his teeth and swinging it.

– *Eeeeer-pqhhhh*, went the wrecking ball-eraser.

His mechanical pencil was aghast. – There goes Big Steel Man!

– *Pqhhhh.*

– Oh no, and Randy River!

– *Pqhhhh.*

– Ack, Tip Top Tailors, Stitches, Northern Reflections, Cotton Ginny. They're all going down, down, down. Where am I going to shop?

– *Pqhhhh. Pqhhhh.*

The eraser bounced happily over the chaos and destruction. – Onto Wal-Mart! The big finale! Ready? *Eeeeer-doing-oing-oing.* Oh no, Wal-Wart has metal walls. Bring out the battering rams. *Boouf. Boouf. Boouf. Boouf.*

– "Attention, shoppers, we are being demolished . . . and you know what that means – once-in-a-lifetime prices! Catastrophic savings! Buy now, before there's nothing left but rubble! Buy! Buy! Buy! Cashiers, stay at your tills until further notice."

– *Boouf. Boouf. Boouf.*

– Ahhhhh! Screams and confusion. Hordes of running terror.

He spun his pencil around his thumb and back. "Okay, King Street. Okay." He wrote down:

Mixed-income housing

Business incentives

Sidewalk repaving failed – other sidewalk initiatives? public art?

Move market outside

He spun his pencil again. He leaned back in his chair. He put an arrow next to mixed-income housing. He spun his pencil. He thought:

```
INT  STUDENT APARTMENT NIGHT


JOHN, 20, a tousled, half-handsome urban plan-
ning student, sits at his drafting table deftly
flipping a pencil around his thumb. Suddenly,
John drops his pencil, takes fistfuls of hair,
throws his head back, and says

                    JOHN
   Oh, God! Why me? Why now? Is it my destiny
   to save King Street? Or is it only a lame
   assignment that will do no good anyway, even
   if I can think of something interesting?
```

He buries his face in his hands, then turns it back up to the ceiling.

> JOHN (CONT'D)
> And how will I know the difference?

John closes his eyes.

SFX — A CIRCLE OPENS IN THE CEILING, LETTING IN A BEAM OF BRIGHT LIGHT.

SOUND of ANGEL CHOIRS.

John opens his eyes astonished. He drops to his knees and grasps his palms together, holding them up. ANGEL CHOIRS trail off like a RECORD BEING TURNED OFF.

> GOD (O/S)
> (in nasal, whiny voice)
> Destiny, shmestiny, just do your work.

Abruptly the circle of light closes, the room is as it was. John has tears of joy streaming down his face. He begins his work with renewed vigour.

He twirled his pencil. He wrote down:
Buskers?
Arcade By-Law?
Theatre/Cabaret
Liquor licensing
Alien invasion.
– Johnny!
– Penguin, thank god. I'm going nuts here. Nuts I say. Nuts!

– Johnny, Johnny, Johnny, you work too hard.

– Incorrect. I don't work hard enough.

– King Street?

– Affirmative.

– King Street is a snap. Mixed-income housing. Bench or two on the sidewalk. Incentives, tax breaks. Swanky jazz/hip-hop/ blues bar naturally, of its own course, takes place of stinky windowless bar for alcoholic men. Coupla trees. Bingo: you've got a sunny, friendly neighbourhood during the day, lively atmosphere at night, safe, interesting, perfect.

– It's all so, so . . .

– Exactly what the prof would do? Liable to get you an A, A-minus? What?

– Boring.

– This? This is exciting compared to most of what planners do.

– I know, I know. I'm doomed.

– You'll get over it. Take a break. Come on down to a surfin' safari.

– Can't. Must plan.

– Johnny.

– No whining.

– Johnny.

– No pleading.

– Whoops Johnny, whoops Johnny, Johnny, Johnny, Johnny.

– All right. If we're going to drink, let's drink.

– Whoops, Johnny!

Back at the drawing board. Mixed-income housing, two park benches, and a street mosaic created by street youth in consultation with a local artist it was. He spun his pencil. But, oh! blowing up the mall was a hard option to give up. Why didn't people come to King Street any more? Because they went to the mall. *Pqhhhh.*

What you needed was a good stock of people nearby. People

on foot, not people with cars. Students. Artists. Old people. All people who needed low-income housing. Co-ops. Converted warehouses. Were there any empty warehouses down there? There were abandoned houses, that was for sure. But who owned them? Could the city buy them for cheap? Or CMHC? Turn 'em into co-ops? He had zoning maps and service maps. They were supposed to have gone on their own mapping expedition for that extra level of detail, but he'd gone with Penguin and they'd never got past the bar.

– Ha! You gotta see this, yelled Pen from his desk.

– What?

– Hamster-breeding Web site.

– Hamsters banging each other in cyberspace?

– They're serious! They got like hamster shows and everything!

– What, like hamster obedience? Hamster retriever trials?

– Conformation. Best of breed. All that.

– Is it going to be your pick of the week?

– Don't know yet.

– Hmm.

Skateboard park. What about a skateboard park? Next to the converted warehouse, which may or may not exist. There had to be an abandoned warehouse down there somewhere. Damn. He'd have to go with the three abandoned houses in a row on Queen Street. Make their conversion into a student competition. Student architects are cheap.

– *I* want to start a Web site, Pen whined.

– We could put a camera in the toilet, John said without lifting his head from the blank page in front of him. Like those net-cams on *Hockey Night in Canada*. Kybo-cam.

– Too scatological, John. You'd get too many weirdos.

– You're one to talk.

– There's also the pure disgust factor. No, it's gotta be, like, totally specific and obscure.

– Breeding habits of the lock-spittle beetle.

– Now you're onto something.

– There's no such thing as a lock-spittle beetle.

– And you're going to let that stop you? Come on, brainstorm, brainstorm.

– I'm already brainstorming King Street. Leave me alone.

Co-op housing. Co-op artists' studio and gallery. Like in Guelph, all those potters. That worked. Skateboard park. Mosaic. Busking festival. He needed some yuppies, though. How would he get yuppies? He wouldn't. They were unplannable. If everything worked, they would just come once it was hip. Insta-yuppie, there was no such thing. They didn't work that way. They waited till the neighbourhood tide had already turned, and then they swarmed up the beach like crabs.

B-minus. Pure B-minus. John swivelled on his stool. – Lithuanian Dadaists, he called out to Pen.

– Lesbians who swim with the whales, said Pen.

John got up and padded to the door of Pen's room. – Soft cheeses north and south, he said.

– Opera lovers of Kansas.

– Gay dwarves of America.

Penguin's eyes went wide.

Welcome to the Gay Dwarves of America Web Site!

Sick of giving head just cause you're the right height for it? Sick of Snow White jokes? Interested in dating other dwarves or just making new friends? Check out our bulletin board. Try our chatline. Or e-mail us. Right now we're just a few gay dwarves, but oh what a mighty force we could become if we only banded together.

- Famous Gay Dwarves
- Dwarf-on-Dwarf Sex

• Health Issues for Gay Dwarves
☞   • Our Fabulous Founders

Click.

Our Fabulous Founders

(photo)

Osborne. I was just another lonely gay dwarf going from one one-night stand to the next until I met Izzy. Finally I feel understood in every way. Finally someone looked into my eyes instead of onto my bald spot and saw my hurting soul. I knew I was gay by the time I was twelve – around the time when other boys' sweet, sweet butts were at eye height. Sometimes I wondered if that was the reason I was gay. But twats were at that height too, so it had to be something more than that.

I was the only dwarf I knew. The only dwarf in my school. The only dwarf on my basketball team. The only dwarf in Scouts. The only dwarf at the Y. Like all dwarves, I thought of running away to the circus. Then I got a scholarship: fashion design, what else? I already designed and sewed all my own clothes. It was a natural step. Karmically not so good though. I mean, there's the hard work, the glamour, the creativity, all that's fine, but really, what's fashion all about? Height! All those models towering over slavering, autocratic designers with Napoleon complexes. Not the place to work out your issues around stature, let me tell you.

Since giving it up and going back to school I am so much more at peace with the world and myself and I want to share that peace and self-love that I've learned with my brothers the world over.

(photo)

Izzy. Hi. I'm Izzy. The Web site was Ozzy's idea. Crazy, huh? But he takes it serious. He's so cute when he's serious. And he's right, too. I never dated another dwarf before him either, I didn't have any dwarf friends. I stayed away from them. We all had our own little place in our group, right? We were the dwarves, they were the norms, we were their dwarves. Mascots. Pets, almost. Doing tricks. (Ha, ha.) And now? Thanks to Ozzy and Gay Dwarves of America, I'm not just my own dwarf among dwarves, I'm my own man among men.

to: gda
from: mel
re: what the?
Are you guys kidding or what? I have ten dollars riding on this.

to: mel
from: gda
re: what?
What.

to: gda
from: mizzd
re: tsk, tsk
scuse me? twats? not a very woman-friendly site, is it, boys?

to: gda
from: anon
re:
Suck my dick, short boy!

to: gda
from: Viola
re: hello out there

Found your Web site a couple of weeks ago. Figured you had to be a couple of college kids joking around. Then thought maybe not. Then thought definitely. I mean, Ozzy and Izzy? Come on! But you never know – truth stranger than fiction and all that. And what the heck. I'm not sleeping, I might as well be typing in the deep of the night. You see, my son is a gay dwarf. Well, he's a dwarf. A Little Person. And I think he's gay, though he hasn't told me yet. And I'm worried about him. At first I thought the problem was girls. Tried to tell him things get better after high school, that the silly ideas there about who can date whom (regardless of how they actually feel) evaporate later on, and people regret that they didn't just date the people they liked instead of the people they matched. If I could go back and say yes to Haji Khan instead of mooning over Vince Gerrard, I'd do it in a flash. Wonder if Vince would do the same with me? (Oh, get over it, honey!) Then I found a copy of Playgirl in his bedroom. (My son's. Not Vince's. Who knows what's in Vince's bedroom.)

So what exactly is it that I'm after? I don't know. Should I tell him that I know? And about your Web site? He's not the only one and all that? Has as much a chance of happiness as anyone? (He does, doesn't he? You're happy, aren't you? You seem happy in your pictures.)

– Did you answer this? John asked Pen.
– What?
– Mom of gay dwarf e-mail. Viola.
– Yup.
– What did you say?
– By all means.
– By all means what?
– Just by all means.

– That's it? That's all you wrote?

– I thought it kind of summed things up. Don't you? Izzy's a man of few words.

– You're Ozzy! I'm Izzy.

– Okay.

– Should've told her we were joking.

– Aren't we sensitive all of a sudden?

– Did you sign it Izzy or Ozzy?

Shrug. Penguin pointed the remote and unmuted the television.

– You're useless, did you know that? Useless.

No reaction.

– What is the Geneva Convention, Penguin said to the TV.

to: Viola
from: Izzy
re: hello out there

Whatever Ozzy wrote you, forget it. He's ... um, unpredictable. I love that about him, except when I hate it. It's never boring around here, I'll tell you that. My advice is: Give him an opening. Your son. Like, rent a gay movie or something (Philadelphia is one my ma loved), and then say how terrible you think people who discriminate are. Something like that. And then if he wants to, he can come out. What do you think? Is it a plan or what?

(p.s. sometimes it *is* boring around here. I can't figure out what's wrong with Ozzy. He doesn't seem to care about anything. He watches TV. He goes to the bar. He eats cereal.)

– You got a D? I don't get it. You're the one who gave me the B-minus spiel.

– They just don't understand genius.

– What did you do?

– Took what was already there and intensified it. Teenage Wasteland, that's the concept. You zone the whole thing for arcades, head shops, and cheap pizza outlets, nothing else, except for a hardware store that sells only discount spray paint, so the kids have easy access to the basic graffiti-making materials. Then, cut the street lighting by half so there's lots of dark corners and doorways for smoking up and making out and destroying property.

– You're fucked.

– The world is fucked, my friend. I'm just along for the ride.

to: gda
from: king
re: howdy
hey, you all. glad to see another dwarf-positive site on the Web. are you all members of the LPA? you should have a link to it. i have told the webmaster about it and he's going to check you out and maybe put a link to yours. you may want to reconsider your word choice in your introductions (i.e., t**ts) if you want a wider audience.

– What did you say to Mom about me? Penguin said.

– *Penfield, darling,* John said, imitating Pen's mother the way they did every time she was mentioned. She didn't call. Why?

– Not Penfield-darling. Pay attention, John. When have I ever called Penfield-darling "Mom"? Penfield-darling, when it's necessary to speak of her at all, is "my mother." I mean the other Mom, dwarf-Mom.

– Oh, her. I don't know, why?

– She's very concerned about me. Wonders if I'm taking vitamins. If I'm going to counselling. Whether I'm having a mid-life crisis. Don't laugh, she's serious.

He snapped his fingers and yelled over the next table at Sal, who was swinging a beer-laden tray from shoulder to table.

– Garçon! 'Nother pitcher.

– Fuck your garçon shit, Pen. Ask me nice.

– Oh, Salvatore, please may we have another pitcher of beer?

– That's better.

– Kay, Johnny. What'd you write?

– I told her Ozzy was depressed.

– You think Ozzy is depressed?

– Who knows what's wrong with Ozzy.

– What's wrong with Ozzy, John?

– Nothing. Nothing.

– What's wrong with Ozzy, John?

– I don't have a fucking clue, Pen, I really don't.

– What's wrong with Ozzy, John?

– Just: does he care? About anything?

– Fuck off. Why should he? He's a useless puke who eats and shits and drinks and watches TV like all the other useless pukes on the planet.

– Ozzy. Not you.

– Why, I oughta . . .

– No, but seriously, are you okay? John asked.

– Who are you, Dr. Joyce Brothers? I'm fine.

– Fine, then. Who's Dr. Joyce Brothers?

Pen's name came up for the pool table. They won it off of two girls who were killing themselves over how bad they were. Their hilarity made John smile inwardly.

– Get out your lipstick, 99, said the cuter one as she aimed a bank shot at the middle pocket, then undershot the cue ball so badly it jumped before jostling the ball it was aimed at.

– Contact, the one with the chopsticks in her hair said. You made contact, that's what's important. They busted up over this.

– Think we should get ourselves some a what they had, John?

Maybe the girls weren't supposed to laugh at that, but they were supposed to notice. They didn't. They were an impermeable set. They were encased in a bubble.

– I don't know, Pen. Looks kinda dangerous.

Pen's next turn he laid a series of loud, vigorous shots that made the balls rattle in the cups as they went down.

Chopstick-Hair crouched so her eye was at table level while the other leaned her face to the same height. Cheek to cheek.

The Bubble of Love, that's what it was. The Bubble of Love. Longing for Angela surged through him, making all John's organs ache, skin included. After the girls flubbed their next shot, he cleared the table and they hung up their cues and doubled away laughing.

– What else did Viola say, John asked as Pen racked the balls.

– Who? said Penguin, chalking his pool cue.

– Viola.

– Who?

– Dwarf-Mom. Did she ask her son if he was gay?

– Ha! How's this for circumlocution? She goes and rents *Philadelphia* and waits for him to say it. Classic, eh?

– And? Does he?

Penguin shook his head. – Falls asleep on the couch. Poor fuck.

– What do you mean?

– You want your mother prying into your sex life? Penguin sank his last ball, then missed the eight.

– Yeah, but it's not just about sex, John said, missing his shot.

– How do you know?

– I read. I watch TV.

Pen rolled his eyes. – Joke, John. Joke.

John blushed. He watched Penguin lean on the table to line up his shot. His T-shirt pulled out of the back of his black jeans. John wondered what it would be like to be attracted to that. If it was Angela instead of Pen leaning over a pool table, he'd be in a drool induced by those hips of hers, he'd be in danger of moaning out loud. Come home, Angela, he thought to himself, looking at Penguin's back that was just his back.

John made himself think of the next step if there were to be one, of putting his hand under Pen's shirt on that piece of skin, of putting his lips on muscle. And then for the length of time between eye-blinks, he felt it. Pen's skin would feel thin, almost not there, and everything underneath his skin, muscle and anger and bitterness would be right there under his hand singing like a hydro line, and

```
INT  CAMPUS BAR NIGHT


Penguin, a tightly wound, skinny guy in black
T-shirt and jeans, stiffens at the touch of his
roommate, John, a tousled, half-handsome urban
planning student. Then he swiftly twists
around, takes John's jaw in his hand, and with
eyes hot as, hot as . . . something hot, he
draws John's lips to his own. The two guys' lips
mash together as if, as if they were starved for
it, as if nothing else existed in the world.
And then . . .
```

Then the feeling, the knowledge was gone and John felt a weird combination of pride that he could have gone that far, and smugness that no one knew what he'd just been thinking, and shame that his whole life he'd let himself be limited by a word. What are ya, a homo? Fuck off, ya homo. In high school he and his friends had run a whole campaign based on it. "Vote for Timbo, he's no homo." Ironically intentioned, sure, but still.

– I'm going home. In his head he heard Homo.

– You do that, said Penguin. He bellowed out the name of the next person on the chalkboard for pool.

Penguin wasn't depressed. He was too wired to be depressed.

John flipped on his computer and checked his e-mail account. One from his brother, one from a friend at Western, a cutesy for-warded message from the same friend's girlfriend. Nothing from Angela. Maybe the phone lines were down in Guatemala. Maybe she was out for a stint in a village with no running water, much less a working computer. Maybe she didn't love him any more.

He checked the GDA account. There were eight pranks along the usual lines, including one that said, "Gay fags must die." He wrote back, "Only gay fags? Not sad ones?" Then he opened the last message.

to: gda
from: king
re: re: re: howdy
>
>Why the fuck would we want a wider audience?
>love, Ozzie
>
Fuck you too, asshole. You guys are so full of shit. You say you got a chatline and you got no chatline, you say famous gay dwarves and then you got pictures of yourselves stuck up there. you're so full of shit. damn right i'm sick of the stupid jokes, every fuckin day another stupid dwarf joke, including you. fuck you, pardon my french.

John wrote:

to: king
from: gda
re: Ozzie's last missive
Sorry.

He was about to queue it. Then he added:

love, Izzy
(p.s. de rien about yr French)

Then he checked the Web site. King was right. If you clicked on "Famous Gay Dwarves" there were the same pictures they'd used for Ozzy and Izzy, one of which they'd got from Pen's year-book, the other from a magazine. He tried clicking on "Dwarf-on-Dwarf Sex." Oo la la, Pen had been busy. Fun with Photoshop.

John stared at the computer for a long while. Then he opened a new file and wrote:

> **to:** viola
> **from:** izzy
> **re:** mea culpa
> Listen, you were right the first time. We are just a couple of college students. We're not gay and we're not dwarves and it was a joke and I'm sorry and I hope things work out for you and your son.

Then he trashed it without sending it. He checked the mail again. There were two new prank e-mails, and one from Viola. She must have been writing right then, at the exact same time he was writing her. Where? Where was she? Somewhere in the States – college students, she said, not university students – but other than that? Was it later or earlier there? Colder or hotter? Did she have a cup of hot chocolate by her computer? A glass of Scotch? Did she have some little personalizing thing on top of her computer? Gumby and Pokey? Mickey Mouse? An Etch-a-Sketch frame for the screen? A picture of her kid? Maybe a picture of the two of them on her screen saver. He wished he knew all of it. He wished she would feel it if he mentally kissed her palm, pulling her hand gently away from where her fingers twisted a strand of hair, opening it with both of his hands and putting his lips gently to the hollow cup of flesh.

Jesus, he was mentally kissing everyone tonight. Angela had to come home soon.

> **to:** gda
> **from:** viola
> **re:** you two

Boy, you two are really something! My advice is you should talk to each other and not me. You remind me of my grandparents when they used to fight. "Tell your grandfather the light in the refrigerator needs changing." "Tell your grandmother the light bulbs are where they've always been." Ozzy's depressed, Izzy's obsessive-compulsive . . .

Nothing new on this end. I keep giving Peter these big openings, he keeps not taking them, and I don't want to force him to say anything if he doesn't want to. Besides, maybe there's a perfectly good explanation for the Playgirl, maybe it's Dolly's (his best friend) and she doesn't want to keep it at her house. Her parents are Baptist and very strict. She spends a lot of time here. Her parents are a little suspicious of me, being a single mother and all, but she told them my husband died, so now they're sympathetic.

I think I should just let things be for a while. As long as Peter knows I love him no matter what, well, what else can I do?

John wrote:

to: viola
from: izzy
re:
Dear Viola. I will miss you. Peter will be fine.

He sent it, turned off his own computer, and then went into the living room and bent down in front of the computer, one of Pen's three, that acted as the GDA server. Index finger hovering over the on-off switch, he blinked several times slowly, then jabbed the button, and listened to the machine's waning hum as it powered down. He took a seat and waited for Pen to come home.

– They don't like being called dwarves. They prefer Little People, John was explaining to Pen the next morning after waking up with couch-print on his face upon Pen's arrival at quarter to seven. Now they were in the kitchen, John watching a small pot on the stove, waiting for it to boil.

– Like that's a whole lot better. "I'd like to thank all the Little People."

– Or person with dwarfism.

– Mr. Fucking PC, Pen said. "We're talking about real people, Pen, real people." Come on, John. They're not real, they're virtual. If they were real, they wouldn't have to rely on the fucking Internet to fill up their dull, empty lives.

– So you're virtual, too.

Pen stopped his pacing around the kitchen. He stared at John.

– Basically. Yeah. He sat down and breathed out a long, boozy stream of air. John decanted boiling water from the pot into a tall glass beaker where it tossed up coffee grinds into a chaotic swirl.

– Your life doesn't have to be dull and empty, Pen.

– God, John. You are just so sickeningly well-intentioned, aren't you? You want me to find God? You want me to find love? You want me to find fulfillment and meaning in my work?

– Yeah. I hope you do. Well, God you can take or leave, I don't care.

– I love that dwarf site, John. It makes me laugh. I crave laughter. Without it I'll die. He laughed. Please let me keep it.

– That's up to you, Pen.

– Now you sound like my Grade Three teacher. You never sound like yourself, you know that? I don't know if there even is a self in there. It's like you've unconsciously sampled the voices of everybody you've met in your life, and I just like push a button and out comes Dr. Joyce Brothers or Angela or my Grade Three teacher – how'd you get her voice, by the way – or Elmer the Safety Elephant or Gloria Steinem or your dad.

– Shut up, Pen.

– Ooo, argument's getting good, now, he's hauling out the big guns. Shut up: the battering ram of the inarticulate. Face it, you have no self. You're selfless. You are. I mean it. You're even trying to help me, you think you're helping me, right? You can't help

me, John. I'm an emotional dwarf. I deserve that site. It's mine.
I'll move out to keep it if I have to. Maybe I'll move out anyway.

– Aw, Pen, don't . . .

– No, seriously. This situation is fucked. Dwarf-Mom is
right, we're like a bickering old couple. We used to have fun and
now we're a bickering old couple and you're the wife. You're the
wife, John, you're the wife.

Pen's face was all screwed up. Water came out the corners of
his eyes. John palmed down the coffee plunger.

– You make no sense, man. You make zero sense.

Now Pen had his head down on the table and John did what
he'd been thinking of doing at the bar. He put his hand on
Pen's back.

– Bed, Pen said, rising and slouching off. John leaned back
against the counter, ran one hand over his face with its rasp of
morning beard, and folded his arms across his chest, inside which
his heart thumpa-thumped. He heard Pen brushing his teeth and
spitting. He heard Pen's door close. He leaned some more.

And then he tiptoed up to Pen's door and put his hand on the
handle, listening. Nothing. He turned the door handle. Pen was
curled on his side on his futon, facing the wall.

– Pen! John whispered. Four steps and he was by the bed. He
crouched. Pen!

No response. John couldn't tell if he was really asleep or not.
And then he didn't care. For as long as it took to spoon behind
Penfield, he didn't care. He put his arm across Pen's waist so his
hand rested against Pen's chest and still didn't know if Pen was
asleep or awake.

Oh, fuck, what if he was asleep? And woke up, going, What
the fuckin' fuck?

What if he was awake?

– John.

Ohfuck. Awake. Fuck.

– What are you doing?

John cleared his throat. – I'm, uh, lying with you.

Pen said nothing.

– You seemed upset.

– Never made you climb into my bed before.

– That's true.

– You could go now.

– Okay. John sproinged to his feet like a jack-in-the-box.

He put on his running shoes and wind jacket and gloves and ran down to King Street. It was Saturday morning on the busiest street in town and there were only handfuls of pedestrians in each block. He ran all the way downtown and then back along the railroad track, through the park with the deer behind their fence, up to the university and then past it, out into the beginnings of the countryside. Fifty kilometres up the road, more or less, and fifty years ago, his father had been born and lived until he was about the age John was now. He stood there looking up it, hands on his hips, until he'd stopped panting. Then he turned around, walked home, went to bed and slept. He and Pen never talked about it again, either the Web site or that morning.

A month and a half later, John went to work as the co-op student at the Goderich Town Planning Department, Pen went to work for the City of Mount Royal, and Angela came home from Guatemala. John and Pen e-mailed each other sporadically, reporting on pickle-butt bosses and sorry-ass co-workers. Originally they had arranged to take the apartment back from the off-stream co-op students currently in it, but there was a room available in a house down the street from Angela's, and John wanted to take it. He was relieved when Pen wrote to say he'd had it with Planning, he didn't know what he wanted to be when he grew up, but a planner wasn't it, and he was taking some time off.

Six months later, John got a postcard from Atlanta, Georgia, with a picture of what looked like an old circus promotion photo, a very tall black man beside a white man of average height in a top hat. In large capital letters, the message said, I'D. Pen, he thought, though the handwriting could have been

anybody's. Who else would send a postcard with a single con-
traction on it? Who else would write to his parents' address?
Over the next month, circus pictures from around the States fol-
lowed, each with one word on them. Postmark Tuscaloosa,
Alabama: Leopard Boy (unhappy-looking black boy with patches
of white skin), message: LIKE. Postmark Amarillo, Texas:
Bearded Lady Triplets, message: TO. Postmark Wichita, Kansas:
Strong Man: THANK. Postmark Las Vegas, New Mexico: The
Marvellous Mexican Midget (drooping mustache, crossed ban-
doliers, twirling six-guns): ALL. Postmark Trinidad, Colorado:
Dapper Dan & His Dancing Dogs (cowboy holding a long pole
with a dog balanced on either end): THE. Postmark Cheyenne,
Wyoming: Fat Lady: LITTLE.

PEOPLE never came. John had thought maybe it would make
sense, finally, of the lot of them, that the postcard saying
PEOPLE would have some image, gay dwarves maybe, that
would tip him off as to what Pen was up to, what the hell he
meant. He put them all up on the fridge, flipping them over a
couple times a day, sometimes arranging them all with the
fronts showing, sometimes all with the backs. He thought of
photocopying the backs and pasting them onto pieces of post-
card-sized cardboard so he could see both fronts and backs at the
same time but he never got around to it.

After another three moves from work-term apartments to
Waterloo apartments and back, Angela finally asked if they really
had to keep them on the fridge any more, and John said, Yes. Yes.
I'm still waiting for PEOPLE. I'll always wait for PEOPLE.

JESSICA GRANT

My Husband's Jump

My husband was an Olympic ski jumper. (*Is* an Olympic ski jumper?) But in the last Olympics, he never landed.

It began like any other jump. His speed was exactly what it should be. His height was impressive, as always. Up, up he went, into a perfect sky that held its breath for him. He soared. Past the ninety- and hundred-meter marks, past every mark, past the marks that weren't really marks at all, just marks for decoration, impossible reference points, marks nobody ever expected to hit. Up. Over the crowd, slicing the sky. Every cheer in every language stopped; every flag in every colour dropped.

It was a wondrous sight.

Then he was gone, and they came after me. Desperate to make sense of it. And what could I tell them? He'd always warned me ski jumping was his life. I'd assumed he meant metaphorically. I didn't know he meant to spend (suspend) his life mid-jump.

How did I feel? Honestly, and I swear this is true, at first I felt only wonder. It was pure, even as I watched him disappear. I wasn't worried about him, not then. I didn't begrudge him, not then. I didn't feel jealous, suspicious, forsaken.

I was pure as that sky.

But through a crack in the blue, in slithered Iago and Cassius

84

and every troublemaker, doubt-planter, and doomsayer there ever was. In slithered the faithless.

Family, friends, teammates, the bloody IOC – they had "thoughts" they wanted to share with me.

The first, from the IOC, was drugs. What did I think about drugs? Of course he must have been taking something, they said. Something their tests had overlooked? They were charming, disarming.

It was not a proud moment for me, shaking my head in public, saying no, no, no in my heart, and secretly checking every pocket, shoe, ski boot, cabinet, canister, and drawer in the house. I found nothing. Neither did the IOC. They tested and retested his blood, his urine, his hair. (They still had these *pieces* of him? Could I have them, I wondered, when they were done?)

The drug theory fizzled, for lack of evidence. Besides, the experts said (and why had they not spoken earlier?) such a drug did not, *could not*, exist. Yet. Though no doubt somebody somewhere was working on it.

A Swiss ski jumper, exhausted and slippery-looking, a rival of my husband's, took me to dinner.

He told me the story of a French man whose hang-glider had caught a bizarre air current. An insidious Alpine wind, he said, one wind in a billion (what were the chances?) had scooped up his wings and lifted him to a cold, airless altitude that could not support life.

Ah. So my husband's skis had caught a similarly rare and determined air current? He had been carried off, against his will, into the stratosphere?

The Swiss ski jumper nodded enthusiastically.

You believe, then, that my husband is dead?

He nodded again, but with less gusto. He was not heartless – just nervous and desperate to persuade me of something he didn't quite believe himself. I watched him fumble helplessly with his fork.

Have you slept recently? I asked. You seem jumpy – excuse the pun.

He frowned. You don't believe it was the wind?

I shook my head. I'd been doing that a lot lately.

His fist hit the table. Then how? He looked around, as if he expected my husband to step out from behind the coat rack. *Ta Da!*

I invited him to check under the table.

Was it jealousy? Had my husband achieved what every ski jumper ultimately longs for, but dares not articulate? A dream that lies dormant, the sleeping back of a ski hill, beneath every jump. A silent, monstrous wish.

Yes, it was jealousy – and I pitied the Swiss ski jumper. I pitied them all. For any jump to follow my husband's, any jump *with a landing*, was now pointless. A hundred meters, a hundred and ten, twenty, thirty meters. Who cared? I had heard the IOC was planning to scrap ski jumping from the next Olympics. How could they hold a *new* event when the last one had never officially ended?

They needed closure, they said. Until they had it, they couldn't move on.

Neither, apparently, could my Swiss friend. He continued to take me to dinner, to lecture me about winds and aerodynamics. He produced weather maps. He insisted, he impressed upon me . . . couldn't I see the veracity, the validity of . . . look here . . . put your finger here on this line and follow it to its logical end. Don't you see how it might have happened?

I shook my head – no. But I did. After the fifth dinner, how could I help but see, even if I couldn't believe?

I caught sleeplessness like an air current. It coiled and uncoiled beneath my blankets, a tiny tornado of worry, fraying the edges of sleep. I would wake, gasping – the *enormity* of what had happened: My husband had never landed. Where was he, *now*, at this instant? Was he dead? Pinned to the side of some unskiable mountain? Had he been carried out to sea and dropped like Icarus, with no witnesses, no one to congratulate him, no one to grieve?

I had an undersea image of him: A slow-motion landing through a fish-suspended world – his skis still in perfect V formation.

Meanwhile the media was attributing my husband's incredible jump to an extramarital affair. They failed to elaborate, or offer proof, or to draw any logical connection between the affair and the feat itself. But this, I understand, is what the media do: They attribute the inexplicable to extramarital affairs. So I tried not to take it personally.

I did, however, tell one reporter that while adultery may break the law of *marriage*, it has never been known to break the law of *gravity*. I was quite pleased with my quip, but they never published it.

My husband's family adopted a more distressing theory. While they didn't believe he was having an affair, they believed he was trying to escape *me*. To jump ship, so to speak. Evidently the marriage was bad. Look at the lengths he'd gone to. Literally, the *lengths*.

In my heart of hearts I knew it wasn't true. I had only to remember the way he proposed, spontaneously, on a chair lift in New Mexico. Or the way he littered our bed with Hershey's Kisses every Valentine's Day. Or the way he taught me to snow-plow with my beginner's skis, making an upside-down V in the snow, the reverse of his in the air.

But their suspicions hurt nonetheless and, I confess, some-times they were *my* suspicions too. Sometimes my life was a Country and Western song: Had he really loved me? How could he just fly away? Not a word, no goodbye. Couldn't he have shared his sky . . . with me?

But these were surface doubts. They came, they went. Like I said, where it counted, in my heart of hearts, I never faltered.

The world was not interested in *my* theory, however. When I mentioned God, eyes glazed or were quickly averted, the subject politely changed. I tried to explain that my husband's jump had made a believer out of me. Out of *me*. That in itself was a miracle.

So where were the religious zealots, now that I'd joined their ranks? I'd spent my life feeling outnumbered by them – how dare they all defect? Now they screamed *Stunt*, or *Affair*, or *Air current*, or *Fraud*. Only I screamed *God*. Mine was the lone voice, howling *God* at the moon, night after night, half expecting to see my husband's silhouette pass before it like Santa Claus.

God was mine. He belonged to me now. I felt the weight of responsibility. Lost a husband, gained a deity. What did it mean? It was like inheriting a pet, unexpectedly. A very large Saint Bernard. What would I feed him? Where would he sleep? Could he cure me of loneliness, bring me a hot beverage when I was sick?

I went to see Sister Perpetua, my old high school principal. She coughed frequently – and her coughs were bigger than she was. Vast, hungry coughs.

Her room was spare: a bed, a table, a chair. Through a gabled window I could see the overpass linking the convent to the school. Tall black triangles drifted to and fro behind the glass.

You've found your faith, Sister Perpetua said.

I couldn't help it.

And then she said what I most dreaded to hear: that she had lost hers.

I left the window and went to her. The bed groaned beneath my weight. Beside me, Sister Perpetua scarcely dented the blanket.

She had lost her faith the night she saw my husband jump. She and the other sisters had been gathered around the television in the common room. When he failed to land, she said, they felt something yanked from them, something sucked from the room, from the world entire – something irrevocably lost.

God?

She shrugged. What we had *thought* was God.

His failure to land, she continued, but I didn't hear the rest. His failure to land. *His failure to land.*

Why not miracle of flight? Why not leap of faith?

I told her I was sure of God's existence now, as sure as if he were tied up in my backyard. I could smell him on my hands. That's how close he was. How real, how tangible, how furry.

She lifted her hands to her face, inhaled deeply, and coughed. For a good three minutes she coughed, and I crouched beneath the swirling air in the room, afraid.

It was a warm night in July. A plaintive wind sang under my sleep. I woke, went to the window, lifted the screen. In the yard below, the dog was softly whining. It was not the wind after all. When he saw me, he was quiet. He had such great sad eyes – they broke the heart, they really did.

I sank to my knees beside the window.

I was content, I told him, when everyone else believed and I did not. Why is that?

He shook his great floppy head. Spittle flew like stars around him.

And now all I'm left with is a dog – forgive me, but you are a very silent partner.

I knelt there for a long time, watching him, watching the sky. I thought about the word *jump*. My husband's word.

I considered it first as a noun, the lesser of its forms. As a noun, it was already over. A completed thing. *A* jump. A half-circle you could trace with your finger, follow on the screen, measure against lines on the ground. Here is where you took off, here is where you landed.

But my husband's *jump* was a verb, not a noun. Forever unfinished. What must it be like, I wondered, to hang your life on a single word? To *jump*. A verb ridden into the sunset. One verb to end all others.

To *jump*. Not to doubt, to pity, to worry, to prove or disprove. Not to remember, to howl, to ask, to answer. Not to love. Not even to *be*.

And not to *land*. Never, ever to land.

DAWN RAE DOWNTON

Hansel and Gretel

A poor woodcutter lived with his wife and his two children on the edge of a large forest. Whoever would remember that it starts like that?

Rollo must have remembered, because that's the first thing he said when he came in last night – "What's this, Hansel and Gretel?" It was another of Mom's potlucks – but this time just Ezra, Viktor, and Galina, because my father got hurt and can't cope, and because it was winter and where we live no one ventures, only squirrels and deer and the occasional skunk, coyotes at night. Rollo came too, for the first time ever; he doesn't like visiting. Viktor and Galina will always come, though, winter or summer. They have that drive over Folly Mountain and in winter they appreciate an early start home, so yesterday everyone came at four, when there was still lots of light. Dad sent me out in broad daylight anyway, saying that a welcoming committee showed some Grace. His little joke. Us living here, that's his joke, that's what I think – though no one wants to know what I think.

Most of the winter I've done all the ferrying and hauling and welcoming between the road and the house. Dad used to carry things here, but since he got hurt it's fallen to me. Out I went yesterday and brought Rollo down the icy garden path, and later the others, too, past the old shed and the woodpile and the sled that we use to tow things between the road and the house. In the morning I'd gone out early and strewn the path with new pine cones and pine needles. It looked better than ashes from the woodstove, and for traction worked just as well. It almost looked romantic, like birds had scattered winter buds.

It was pretty, but a guy like Rollo, he'd never say.

Rollo just picked his way over the ice on his ground-down heels, muttering, clanking the wine bottles in his knapsack. What a surprise that he came at all. Mom and Dad have talked about him my whole life, but seldom are we actually subjected to him. Mom and Dad like him, though. He's for contemplating – that's what Mom says. He edits an art magazine; he's rude and stuck-up and so tall and above it all, but worn down at the heels so badly that he seems to tip even when he doesn't drink too much. Most of the afternoon I had the opportunity to compare his shoes to Viktor's, since they sat on the couch side by side and stretched their legs out, ready to spring up and box each other to a pulp at the slightest provocation. Maybe Viktor and Galina should have seen it coming, should have gulped their after-dinner tea and left before any of it started. Galina, that is. Viktor couldn't have seen anything. Maybe he should have smelled it.

Viktor is almost as tall as Rollo, but filled out. He's solid, steady, as if he's been walking a long time, walking and watching in the falling light, and now he's found his way and stopped. He looks like Sean Connery and talks like him too, although he's from Krakow. He has perfect shoes. A guy like that who can't see his own teeth to brush them any more, and he has perfect shoes. Leather shoes with laces, in a place like ours. I hardly bother to tie up my hair any more, even now that it's got so long, and I can't imagine when I last saw any of my barrettes. But no old running shoes for Viktor, no lined galoshes. Over their shoes he and Galina wore their strap-on ice cleats. "Gives a blind man a little poise," Viktor said, and everyone said "yes, yes" too quickly, as if Viktor's blindness was as common as the shoes on all our feet.

Rollo's feet are flippers. Like everything about him from his crazy hair to his Coke-bottle glasses, they make him look like the Creature from the Deeps. I guided Rollo and his flippers through the mudroom, past all the stacked firewood.

"Bring your boots in, Rollo," I said to him, like we say to everybody, but he's the only one who's ever said this back: "Why, Grace? Will they go somewhere if I leave them out?"

I don't know, maybe people like Rollo like having cold feet.

And then he came in and saw how everything was jammed together into our two little rooms downstairs, the walls finished with Dad's rough, hand-planed boards and Mom's storybook paint job, lavender with Wedgwood blue trim. Maybe it didn't say *sweet* at all. Maybe it said *poor*.

Maybe that's what Rollo saw, how poor and precious we were. "What's this?" he said, waving his cigarette. "Hansel and Gretel?"

Everyone hates Rollo's smoking. I was glad of it, though, the way it disguised my own nips into the woods with Amanda. She'd skated over from her house down the road and waited for me just inside our stand of spruce. She had her papers and her pouch of Drum, even a big box of Redbird matches in case we got a lot of wind. Between guests arriving we'd grab a smoke. While we waited for Ezra to rock his Toyota out of the snowbank we had two each, hiding there in the trees, watching. Then I went to help push, Ezra's wheels spinning, my head spinning from the nicotine.

It's just one of the rotten jobs I've been stuck with since Carson left on her scholarship, leading guests down the garden path to the house from the road where they leave their cars. And then taking them back in the pitch dark. That's the part I really hate, because I'm afraid of the dark. Not the coyotes so much, just the dark itself. You look and look and what was there is not. Will it ever come again? In the dark, that's when I lose my balance.

But I'm glad for Carson. Opportunity found her here in the woods, and it knocked. She was always good at school, but all the same it's not like so many opportunities come our way. It's like Rollo also said, panting down the trail behind me: "Bet you don't get a lot of door-to-door salesmen down here."

So no, I don't begrudge Carson. But now hear this – I'm not doing her job forever. She better be back here once spring term ends, not gallivanting over to Paris or the Alps or down to Tunis with the rest of them when there's a school break. She better not be escaping again.

Ezra finally got his car off the ice. He saw Rollo the minute he was through the door from the mudroom, his boots in his hand. "Oh," he said. "It's you."

Ezra and Rollo hate each other, but my mother is always hoping for the best and so she invites them over together all the time. Rollo never comes, but Ezra is a regular. He served in Vietnam willingly, and that makes him something of a curiosity to my parents. My father had a low draft number and joined the Quakers, but he never got proper CO clearance and on one of his many trips to Canada all those years ago he just didn't find his way back home.

Rollo, on the other hand, is a bona fide draft dodger. He and I share a birthday – because of that, my parents made him my godfather – and he's pointed out that if I'd been born a boy in the U.S. with that birthday, between 1944 and 1950, like he was, I'd be one too.

"No, I would have served," I said again last night, as I always do when he starts in on me. Pick on someone your own size, I always want to say, but he doesn't need inviting.

"You would have died, you mean." Thirty-five years across the border in another sovereign state entirely and Rollo can still go on about this. He said if you got drafted you were more likely to die than if you'd just bit the bullet and enlisted. Draftees usually joined the ground forces where the heavy casualties were.

"That's the same with any war," I said. Like I knew. But to hear Rollo tell it, the whole of the navy, the air force, and the marines sat on deck chairs on the beach at Nha Trang and waited the conflict out, now and then renewing their sunscreen. The officers especially.

"Any war's the same as any war," my mother said.

Rollo said if you had a number below 196, sooner or later it came up. Anybody with a higher number was safe. Rollo said Bill Clinton didn't have a low number. He didn't have a number at all because he was old enough to have had to register for the draft before the lottery started in 1969, and who knew what that boded. He went right out and got himself a 2-S deferment, a student deferment. The big deferments were 2-S and 4-F, the medical exemption, "for a pimple on your ass if you knew the right people."

But never mind Clinton, Rollo said. The draft lottery wasn't a lottery anyway, not for anyone. It wasn't random. All the days of the year – even February 29th for leap year – all three hundred and sixty-six dates written on three hundred and sixty-six cards went in sequence into the barrel. It wasn't spun enough to mix the cards up and make the dates truly random, and most of the later dates stayed on top, so that the numbers drawn out first – the low numbers – were likely to be for birthdays in the second half of the year.

Where was Bob Barker when you needed him, someone who could have done this right? Where were Janice and Holly and Anitra? Vanna?

The birthday Rollo and I share is in late October, and our draft number would have been seven. *Seven.* When I think about it my throat gets dry. My number *would have been* seven, I should say. Rollo's number *was* seven. No wonder he ran. No wonder his shoes are all worn down, from running. No wonder he's thin.

The woodcutter did not have much food around the house, it continues – it really does – *and when a great famine devastated the entire country, he could no longer provide enough for his*

family's daily meals. "*Early tomorrow morning,*" *said his wife,*
"*we'll take the children out to the forest where it's most dense.*
They won't find their way back home, and we'll be rid of them."

Well, we've never been that hungry, what with all Mom
knows about edible weeds, and how resourceful she is. Once she
swerved to miss a rabbit in the road, but hit it anyway. Waste
not, want not – the skin came off like a glove pulled back, and
she used herbs from her pots on the windowsill, braising it a
long time. With winter rabbits you have to do that, she said as
if she were an authority. Rabbits are tough and gamey until
they start feeding on roots and plants in the spring. There's a six-
week period where they're patchy-looking, turning from their
winter white back to brown. Right afterwards – that's the time
to get them.

At our Sunday potlucks we see things we never see otherwise
– shrimp in the salad, raisin bread tied into challah loaves,
apricot chutney. Broccoli, sweet peppers in red, yellow, orange.
On their own, my family believes only in winter vegetables –
potatoes, sweet potatoes, turnips, squash. Cabbage too; always
cabbage, always boiled. It's unecological to eat anything out of
season. Think of the costs of shipping from California and
Florida. Think of the labour costs, the energy costs, how unnat-
ural it all is.

Yum.

I complain to my parents about what we eat. It's natural,
they say. So what? I say. It could be worse, they say; think of this:
Ymir, the four-mouthed giant of Norse mythology, had to drink
directly from the four udders of Audhumia the cow – and she
herself ate nothing but frost. For her roadkill rabbit my mother
won the *Who's Got the Weirdest Mom?* contest I had on that
year with Amanda. Her mom didn't even come close. All she did
was wear a bathing cap in the shower, not a proper shower cap.
We don't even have a shower, but Amanda thinks her mother's
bathing cap makes her weird. We don't even have hot water in
summer, only in winter when we heat it off our woodstove.

Who's Got the Rudest Guests? I wanted to run out last night and tell Amanda we'd won that one too. Rollo the draft dodger has celiac sprue – but not when it comes to pie. He may be bloated and gassy, but not around sweets. Mom passed around her eleven-inch apple and cranberry deepdish straight out of the warming oven, and taking the server in both hands while Galina, next to him, held the dish, he levered a huge hunk out onto his plate. He ran his fingers along the blade of the server, then his tongue. He didn't care if he cut himself, he didn't care who might have needed the knife after him. Rollo just doesn't care. He blames his celiac sprue on the war, too, saying you have to have the genetic predilection for it but also a triggering event. An event like *stress*, he says, a *precipitate*.

Rollo likes to sound scientific. I think he wishes he were in science journalism, not art, and hopes that people will forget it's *ArtSmart* he runs. He says celiac sprue is just more fallout from American imperialism, and that even from far away, here in Canada, he would have sued the U.S. government for the loss of his health if he'd thought there was any point. But there's no point to anything. There's nothing you can change. When someone challenged the randomness of the draft lottery in court, for instance, a judge threw the case out.

Rollo talks numbers. He's precise; he's an editor. You can't change anything, it seems, but you can talk it to death. There was a statistically significant correlation between where your birthdate fell in the year and your likelihood of getting drawn, getting a low number. A correlation of -.28, when it should have been zero.

"It's, like, minus twenty-eight outside right now," Galina said, pulling back the curtain, the one Mom constructed out of a stained old tablecloth from the remnants table at Goodwill. Galina's forever holding things for other people. Holding things back so that they can see, holding things up so that they can serve themselves. Outside, the light was just starting to fall. Galina let the curtain drop. Maybe she sensed it then – the heavy weather, the turbulence climbing the air like an animal on a drape.

Last summer I followed the fragrance of roses into the garden. I bent and swept the fallen petals up in my fingers, and I stuck my hand right into the jellied, rotting eye of a dead skunk.

Maybe if Galina and Viktor could have set down their pie forks right then, gulped their tea, and left before any of it started. Maybe they could have been well over Folly Mountain by the time Rollo got so drunk.

"I was born on February 2," Viktor said. "What would my draft number have been?" Does he know he looks like Sean Connery? Even though he's blind, maybe he knows. He said it just like he was in a movie.

Rollo bristled. He took off his Coke-bottle glasses, wiped them in his dirty sweatshirt, and replaced them on his flat red nose. "It's not a parlour game," he said.

"But you could figure it out if you wanted to."

"Rollo can figure anything out. You know Rollo." It was Ezra, tucking a last bite of cranberry and apple into his mouth. He brushed the front of his shirt carefully with one hand, collecting the crumbs in the other. He'd spoken for the first time in ages. With Rollo, how could anyone get a word in edgewise? Now Ezra had thrown a glove down, *smack*.

My mother was distraught. She's a bona fide Quaker, one my father found when he needed help filing his objector status. She came from a family of Quakers, and they from a family before her. My mother has Quaker papers that go back generations. She believes fences can be mended, that Ezras and Rollos can come together, that we can all get along. She cut across the table through the men's squabbling as deftly as if it had been a frozen pond and she'd donned Amanda's skates.

"That was wonderful phyllo, Gally," she said. "You're such a talent." Gally and Viktor had brought bean salad, spinach and feta phyllo, cheesecake from the Harrowsmith cookbook.

Viktor made that. He's quite a cook. It had a whole wheat crust, but living in the woods with the woodcutter and his wife who freezes lamb's quarter and purslane from the weed fields for winter greens, I'm used to that sort of thing.

Only Rollo hadn't brought something. Cooking, that's the sort of thing he's above. Even stopping at the store in the village to get a few rolls – he's above that too. Except for the liquor store. He *had* stopped there.

"Carson," I said out of the blue. "Carson would have had a high draft number, I bet. She's always escaping."

Everyone looked up at me. Like Ezra, I hadn't been saying much. It was true, I thought. How do you escape a life? It was something Carson knew, something Rollo and Dad and Bill Clinton knew, even something Mom knew when she quilted on her lap late at night and hummed her hymns. She was in her greying years, and it was never clear how much a part of the world she was. She knew how to leave. It was something I had to find out.

"We weren't *escaping*," Rollo sniffed. "We were *objecting*. We were drawing our line in the sand, taking our stand. Even Clinton –"

"Yes?" Ezra asked, but he and Viktor both waited. Viktor had been sitting quietly, listening. He hadn't eaten much.

"I was only going to say, even Clinton held anti-war protests where he was."

"And where was he?"

"Oxford, of course. Everybody knows he was at Oxford."

"He escaped there."

"He *went* there. Really, Ezra," Rollo said. "Give it up."

"Well. I just thought given all that noble escaping and line-drawing he was doing he might have gone somewhere charitable, somewhere he could be useful. How was it we used to say it? Somewhere he could *make a difference*. The slums of Calcutta, maybe. To empty slop pails for Mother Theresa."

"They didn't have them then."

"Slop pails?"

"Slums. For Westerners."

"They didn't have slums in Calcutta in the sixties? What, they're a modern invention?"

"I merely meant to suggest, Ezra, that Westerners didn't go to India then."

"The Beatles did. Mia Farrow."

"Mother Theresa wasn't well known. There wasn't anything there then."

"Any what? Cachet? There wasn't any celebrity in it?"

"Infrastructure, I meant."

"*In*frastructure?" Ezra sounded bewildered.

"Carson just wants to get an education at Oxford," I said. "That's why she went as soon as the scholarship came along. She figures with a degree from Oxford the world is her oyster."

"Exactly," said Ezra, eyeing Rollo as if there'd been a struggle between them over some bone and he'd come away with it in his teeth. "Carson and Clinton."

"Grace," my mother said. "Help us clear away the dishes?" She was angry with Ezra, of all people. She didn't think much of politicians. Rollo had opened the door on a throng of hangers-on with high numbers or no numbers at all and now Ezra had dragged them in, people she would never invite into her ginger-bread house, not out of the coldest wind. How could our Carson be like Bill Clinton?

"Viktor was out shovelling roofs today," Galina said. She was a gentle woman, a good woman, we all said, for Viktor to go blind with. When I met her coming down the garden path I'd planned to tell her what a good thing it was they'd arrived so early, before the coyotes moved in for the night. City people are always afraid of the wrong things. But I couldn't bring myself to do it. She'd been reading something to Viktor and still had her glasses on, taking them off only when I hailed from below. She'd screwed her eyes up to see who it was – *You look so much like your mother, Grace. You're getting so tall. You're so pretty, just like your mom.* She always said that. When I reached her, the softness in her face, the heed about her eyes – my coyotes ran away.

"He wore his ice cleats going up the ladders," Galina said. She squeezed Viktor's hand. It was a feat.

"We have a few rental properties," Viktor explained to Ezra. "They've all got ice dams up the ying yang. Leaks everywhere. Tenants, you know. They want things fixed right away. Can't wait. We haven't fixed our own leaks yet, and I'm up on all their roofs. Blind as a bat yet, legally blind."

Rollo was swirling wine in his glass. Oblivious, he'd already spilled it on the tablecloth, the one that had once been an old bedsheet from Goodwill but had looked pretty enough till now.

"That's right, I'd forgotten," he said, pushing his chair back hard into our pine plank floor, scratching it. "Viktor's a property owner. A landlord." He drank his glass down and set it sharply on the table. "A slum landlord."

An hour later, Rollo and Ezra were still at it. "Yeah, surveillance, right?" Rollo spat at Ezra. They'd carried on yelling and shouting about the war in the living room, about who had the most virtue then and who was more evolved because of it now. Ezra might have done something *nefarious* during the war. It was one of those words I loved the sound of, and about which my mother said she really couldn't comment.

Now Mom sat with Galina out of the way, on the futon on the far side of the room, looking at the last batch of photos Carson had sent.

"Electronics and communications and feeds from the field my ass," Rollo hissed. "ITT stuff. You went down to Chile after that, did you, and helped overthrow Allende?"

"I went to the DEW Line after that," Ezra said icily. "To chill. You should try it sometime, Rollo."

"I hope this is a mistake," Mom said to Gally, passing her Carson's close-up of her Oxford boyfriend's crotch. "Sweetheart, do you think it's a mistake?"

She looked meaningfully at my father, then anxiously at Ezra and Rollo at the end of the room, but my father turned away. Resigned, my mother turned back to the pictures. Carson and her friends had made one trip to the Mediterranean already, during their Christmas break. These were pictures of a street party in Napoli on Christmas Day. Some of the boys had the girls' dresses on. That was how I knew Adrian was the boyfriend; he was the one wearing Carson's favourite summer dress. I'd worn that dress, the one time she'd let me. It had been the first Christmas ever that Carson hadn't been here with us – now it turns out her dress hadn't been there either but on some throwaway guy halfway around the world in the sun – and Mom looked pale for days, trying to get used to it. I slept in Carson's bed a couple times but gave it up. It just felt wrong to me, coarse and cold and with the soft spots all in the wrong places. There we were in our woodcutter's Christmas without her; there she was, off in the Mediterranean, shooting Adrian's crotch.

I looked over Galina's shoulder at the picture again. "It's a walking stick," I said. "Right there, running parallel to the fly."

"A *what*?"

"A walking stick. Those bug things, you know. Next to his zipper, I mean. That's why Carson took the picture. Adrian had an exotic bug on him."

"Well," said my mother. "She might have written something on the back. She's written things on the back of some of the other ones."

"Who's the other nation?" From across the room it was Ezra again, sourly, to Rollo.

"The First Nations," Rollo said. They were on to native rights now, since Ezra had been in the North on the DEW Line. "All I'm saying is how'd you like to be the second nation the first is lording things over?"

"I thought you said they *were* the First."

"Shut up," Rollo said, pouring out more wine, splashing it on Mom's batik rug. "Just shut the fuck up."

"Rol. Hey, man. No need for that." It was my father, dis-
tantly, from across the room.

Rollo whirled around, his glass spraying again. "You shut
the fuck up too."

My father blanched; I felt for him, as if I'd taken the blow,
been hit in the chest.

"Here, hold this a moment, will you?" Viktor said. He'd been
quiet since Rollo's slum landlord remark back at the table, but
now he rose, put on his coat and gloves though he waved Galina
back to her seat. He picked up the cast iron kettle from the top
of the woodstove and handed it to Rollo, who was too drunk to
know better.

"Son of a bitch!" Rollo screamed, flinging it across the room
where it slammed into Dad's leg, the bad one. Dad screamed too.
Everyone was screaming; screams lit up the house like a rocket
and outside I heard Lucky, Amanda's collie, barking through the
woods. Rollo was grappling on the floor with Viktor, and Ezra
threw himself on both of them.

"Shut up, shut up, shut *up*!" Ezra cried, pounding down with
his fists.

It was a small space for all that. Galina and my mother, on
their futon at the perimeter, drew their feet in as if a drain had
overflowed and grey water was coming straight at them. My
father was gripping his leg where the kettle had hit him, and his
face had gone very white. His head hung back so that his jaw par-
alleled the ceiling, but it yawned open as if a hinge had jammed.
It was his way of screaming. I thought I should hold on to the
lamps, the bookshelves with their knick-knacks. It was what I'd
do if an earthquake hit, if a plane flew too low. We didn't have
enough, God knew, to lose any of it now.

Rollo, Ezra, Viktor writhed on the floor. Viktor pulled open
Rollo's mouth in the kind of move you'd see on Wild World of
Wrestling, and Rollo bit down hard on Viktor's thumb. Maybe
that was a wrestling thing too. Viktor drew his other hand out
from under the three of them and slapped Rollo in the face. It

was womanish, silly in the midst of all the muscles. For a moment, they all stopped, surprised.

I sprang to the stove and pulled out a piece of burning wood with the tongs, waving it at them.

"Get out!" I screamed. We all choked with the smoke.

"Who?" It was Viktor, looking up at nothing. When he looked at you he didn't really find you any more.

"Whoever." I looked at my mother. "Mom? Who should go? Whose fault is this?"

But Mom only waved at her face with a hand, struggling to push herself up from the futon with the other. Beside her, Gally had shrunk down to nothing, Carson's photographs still fanned in her hand like magic cards.

"Dad?" I said. He'd hung his head down. His hands were still gripping his leg, as if in some marvellous sports feat, just for the style points, he might pick it up, cast and all, and heave it over his head. He didn't look at me. His leg was his world lately, and never more so than now. Seeing him I felt a thickness in me, as if something had iced over and couldn't flow. If I went outside, I thought, I still might catch the 5:45 to Gatwick. Transatlantic flights went right over our heads every night, en route to Gander and then east. I liked to stand under the trees and look up through the boughs at the contrail of the 5:45, way up there in a high sky turning to pewter. I imagined travellers up there, looking down on the vast ocean. I'd feel something seeping out of me, something I didn't have a word for, like an odour you might have trouble describing but would know in a second.

"Here," said Viktor, reaching up to me from the floor where he lay. "Grace. Give me a hand."

"You know Dolly Parton, Viktor?" I was at his side now, out the door and down the steps, watching his breath fume white in the night air. We were walking fast, away from the house, panting together. "At the end of high school everyone was asked their plans for the future and Dolly Parton said she was going to

Nashville to be a star. Everyone laughed at her and she couldn't understand why?"

"I'm not laughing," he said. His breath fumed again. The fight had been a strain on him. How much of a strain could a blind man take?

"Well no. Not after that, I guess," I said. I wanted him to ask me what I was going to do after high school. I was nearly there, after all. I'd do something grand, something better than Carson. I'd have made something up if he'd asked, and later it would come to me, the real thing I'd do. But he didn't ask. We just walked in silence. We were going ahead on the trail up to the cars, to anywhere. Beside me on the path he was surefooted, stepping out of the range of my flashlight. I was gasping still from the scene in the house, and I had to huff to keep up. Carson had always ferried Viktor and Galina before. I'd never seen him on his feet like this, hadn't known his power. It was that getting on in life he'd been doing, that getting somewhere. He was fit, determined. What had I expected, a Stevie Wonder bobbing, an old man in Ray Charles glasses tapping his way through our ice forest with a cane?

"The food was good," I said.

Beside me, his shoulders shrugged.

"The cake," I tried again. "That was yours?"

"Right."

I was imagining Sean Connery saying it in a movie. *Right.* "You can read recipes? You can read cookbooks?"

He shrugged again.

"Viktor," I said. "You're so fast. It's the first time I've ferried you."

"Charon," he said. "Ha. Styx. Did you know, Gracie, that the river Styx flows nine times around the infernal regions?" There was something in his voice. I hadn't heard it in Sean Connery.

"Back in the house, you mean."

"It's not hell just back in the house. It's hell everywhere."

"What's wrong with Ezra and Rollo, then?"

"I don't know," he said, holding back a branch for me. How had he seen it? "What's wrong with your mother and your father? I might ask the same of them."

"My father broke his leg." Didn't Viktor know?

"Did he? Or did he just hang around too long at the scene of his resurrection? Did they all?"

"His resurrection?"

"Canada. Back to Canada, back to the land. Some fairy tale." There, that thing in his voice again.

"Viktor," I said. "Do you think it's Hansel and Gretel here?"

"Hansel and who?"

"Gret –"

"Never mind. Which one are you? Carson's Hansel, is she, gone off ahead to leave the trail of breadcrumbs?"

"I just thought –"

"You know what, Grace? *The Great Gatsby*, you know that? It started out as the story about a boy who killed his mother."

"Right," I said. *The Great Gatsby* had Robert Redford in it, and Mia Farrow who had gone to India with the Beatles. Amanda's mother had a video collection.

"That's all you've got to say, 'Right'? You should watch what you're thinking, Grace. Everyone should. You should nurse it into something better, not something worse." He shrugged a shoulder back in the direction of the house. "You see what happens when you don't."

"Well," I said, trying to turn this over. Back at the house, a door banged, someone swore; the sound sprang up at us through the dark. It alarmed me again and I skidded on the path, on the trajectory of the trouble. My adrenalin flew up. What if I broke an ankle? I imagined myself blind like Viktor, trying not to break an ankle on this damn journey to my lousy friends in their lousy fairy-tale house. "Do you think we live in a gingerbread house?" I asked.

"I think you should honour your father and your mother." He was gruff now. "Your mother is an honourable woman. Nothing like the woman in the gingerbread house."

"Viktor," I said. "Has anyone told you that you look just like Sean Connery?"

He stopped beside me and sighed. He stared past me but I knew he meant to look at me, squarely in my face. His blindness couldn't tell him just where that was. Was he glaring at me? Was I imagining it? The whole evening, my life here in the woods, that Viktor could be so blind and yet save the day – it was getting to be too much. While I'd stood there brandishing my live split, raining its embers all over my mother's batik, he'd pulled himself to his feet at the end of my hand, stepping over Ezra and Rollo, and dusted off his knees. He'd taken the split in a glove and walked it to the door, into the mudroom past Rollo's flipper shoes and out the front, where he threw it in the snow. Together, we'd followed it, closing the front door on the heat of the house and stepping out into the cooling dusk.

"Viktor," I'd said on the path once we were out the door, "your glove's ruined."

He had shrugged. "Well, I'll never know, will I?"

We'd missed the jet. There was one star overhead. It looked ridiculous. "Where are the rest?" I asked him. He was the kind of man you could ask.

"Desultory," he said.

It wasn't a word I knew.

"You should," he said. "Unconnected. Aimless."

Why should I have known? Did he think those things of me?

"The stars only connect in constellations because we think we can see that they do. We connect the dots." It had gotten raw, and he pulled his gloves down tighter over his hands. I snugged my chin down into my sweater. We walked, and then I asked him those things about cooking and about looking like Sean Connery, and that was when he stopped and gave me that glare, or a blind approximation of it. Even glowering at someone properly depends on knowing how it's going over.

"You lead a charmed life, Grace," he said. "Don't you ever forget it. But you have, haven't you? I'm too late, telling you that."

"I don't know." The rabbit, the edible weeds. Christmas in Napoli. Now, fistfights in the house. My father. My father, nothing. I wanted to agree with Viktor, or disagree, if that was what he wanted. *It's not too late for me, it's not too late* – I could say that. Suddenly it was crucial that he like me, that I please him, that we be on the same side. It was the side of heroes.

"Grace." He took me by the shoulders. His glove was streaked with carbon. "You think you know things now. You get a bit older and you're going to find out that you knew nothing at all – that there was *nothing* you knew." He waved his hands wide as if to demonstrate nothingness. It was so black by then that he was waving into nothing, into everything the night had swallowed up. "You'll be staggered at how far off you were," he said. "Blindsided. But you never mind that. Okay, Gracie? Promise me that's not what you'll mind." I stared up into his eyes, into everything and nothing. "Promise me you'll remember that you *were* sure about everything, that it was possible. Remember how it made you feel. Like you could do anything, right? Tell me you won't forget."

"I won't forget." I had no idea what he was talking about. Was it a hero's talk? Lucky bounded out of the woods at us, as if she could bring a dog's view to bear, and she yipped and danced around Viktor as if she'd found an old friend. He looked around, as if he could, and finding nothing for her he stripped off his glove and threw it long and hard, like a flat stone over an ocean.

That was the wonderful thing – that's what I'm remembering this for. Not Rollo, not Ezra, not the firebrand in my hands. Not even my father. It was the way Viktor threw that ruined glove blind, so sweet and sure, a perfect pitch in the dark. Lucky ran off in the woods, happily charging after anything that belonged to a friend, and Viktor headed back down the path to get Galina.

Last summer, clouds hung above our house and brought in tremendous rain. I missed our hot water. It was an afternoon, I was alone, and I stripped off and ran out into the torrents, the white, cool sheets, up the path and into the garden through the heavy corn. That late in the season the corn was nearly as tall as I was. If anyone had come I could have hidden in it, but only Lucky came. She joined me that day too, bounding around me and springing up and yipping as I ran flying over the long grass, over the garden mounds, prancing, soaked, flinging water into the beans from the ends of my hair and my fingertips. I ran and ran, and every step brought me nearer the place where the rest of my days I'd stand and watch, shivering in the cold and turning blue, where never in my life would I do that again, or anything like it.

"Now we really must get on our way," Viktor had said. I stood on my little hill of ice and watched him go. My flashlight hung down, blooming a small glow around my toes, lighting my piece of the darkness.

"The light," I called after him, holding it out, but without looking around at me he waved me back. It seemed to me he might sashay, he might dance down the path blind, and then he disappeared into the night.

HILARY DEAN

The Lemon Stories

Mrs. Lemon ruined her husband's life. He retaliated by turning her house inside-out in the middle of the night. She was awakened by a spring breeze lifting her nightgown and the sound of the neighbours criticizing her taste in wallpaper. Mrs. Lemon became very self-conscious and hurried to cover herself in her peach kimono.

She watched Mr. Lemon come riding down the street on his brown palomino. He dismounted in front of the house.

"Hello, Life-ruiner," he said.

"It was an accident," she replied. "I never thought you would resort to mythological activities."

"Yes, well, revenge," he explained. "At any rate, I am quite upset. I am suffering as no human being on this earth has ever suffered or ever will in the future."

"That is terrible," said Mrs. Lemon.

She offered him tea, which he declined.

"I am, in fact," he continued, "about to cry."

They both waited, in vain, for his eyes to moisten.

"Never mind," said Mrs. Lemon. "How is the horse?"

"As you can see," said Mr. Lemon, gesturing wildly at the animal, "the horse is quite miserable."

"And your mother?"

"She is well."

"And your mother's horse?"

"Dead."

"I'm sorry."

"Please don't pretend to care. That horse's death is *my* tragedy. I loved that horse like he was my own son!"

"I thought that horse was a mare . . ."

"You don't know anything."

"I thought I watched that horse give birth."

"Purely hallucination."

"So vivid . . ."

Mr. and Mrs. Lemon sat for a while on the grass in composed silence.

"I assure you," said Mrs. Lemon, "it was a complete accident."

"It was a horrible thing you did."

"Yes, I am a horrible kind of person."

"Obviously."

Mr. and Mrs. Lemon were sitting on a porch in the middle of nowhere, rocking back and forth in matching chairs and mutual apathy. It was a beautiful day.

"We have grown old," said Mrs. Lemon. She reached down to pat the dog at her feet, but it had run away several weeks before.

"Yes," answered Mr. Lemon.

"The children have grown and left us. They have their own lives now, I suppose."

"We had no children."

"Of course we did, darling. They climbed trees and skinned their knees and got into all sorts of hijinks."

"There were no children. There were no hijinks."

"I seem to recall hijinks. And much nurturing."

"You had a garden. It was lovely."

They looked up at the clouds for some time.

"I ovulated often."

"Did you?"

"All the time."

"I never noticed." Mr. Lemon squinted into the sunlight. He held his hands out before him and studied them at length.

"I am wrinkled," he said. "I am quite wrinkled everywhere."

Mrs. Lemon looked at him and nodded.

"I have shrunken inside my own skin," he said. "I do not recall exactly when it happened."

She shrugged.

"You are still a very handsome man."

"Yes. But that is no consolation."

In the distance, a figure was approaching in an enthusiastic and frolicsome manner.

"The dog has come back," said Mr. Lemon.

"I am glad," said Mrs. Lemon. "I have missed it terribly."

"You have always suffered from an excess of sentimentality."

"I would not call it 'suffering.'"

"I love you," said Mr. Lemon as they strolled down Lover's Lane holding hands.

"Yes," she replied. "I am lovable."

"I have grown tired of your courtship rituals," she said.

"Have you?"

"I have."

"What of the love letters?"

"Burned for fuel."

"The lace handkerchiefs?"

"Tourniquets for wounded soldiers."

"The elm tree that I carved our initials into?"

"I chopped it down this morning."

"How could you?"

"With an axe."

"You are clever," he said. "Yet you cannot escape my love. It is as powerful as a mighty squid."

"That may be," she answered, "but society forbids our union, and the power of society remains uncontested."

"My dear," he said, looking into her eyes, "we shall run far away, and we shall run very fast."

"In which direction?"

"In any you choose."

"I choose east."

They had reached the end of the lane. She watched a butterfly alight upon his hat. He studied a mosquito sucking blood from her forearm.

"Then you will marry me?" he asked.

"Yes," she replied. "I shall wear white, as I have managed to remain virginal, despite many near-fuckings."

"I will wear my best and only suit."

"It will be beautiful."

"Yes. Beautiful."

She turned to leave.

"Do you love me?" he asked.

"Yes," she answered, "as my nightmares predicted."

"We get along well," said Mr. Lemon, "do we not?"

"We have grown used to each other," said Mrs. Lemon. "We cannot help it."

"But we used to fight so often, and with such passionate intensity. What has happened to that sweet flame of anger and destruction?"

"It has died, along with my will to be your constant opponent."

"But why?"

"It is easier to ignore you when you are being something of a prick."

Mr. Lemon blinked several times in indignation.

"My dear, you are not always a fluffy pink cloud yourself," he said. "I recall the time you slapped my face in front of all those people."

"I had to do it. You were hysterical."

"I was in the middle of a dance contest."

"I could not tell the difference. Must I apologize for one mistake forever?"

"It was humiliating."

"I am sorry. I am filled with a deep and everlasting regret."

"Now you mock me with your sarcasm. That trophy should have been mine. I was the best," he said wistfully.

"You still are the best," she said, "the best at baiting your poor wife. I will argue no longer."

"Perhaps another time, then," said Mr. Lemon. He sighed. "I cannot stand being ignored."

"We get along well," said Mrs. Lemon. "It is a good way to get along."

Mrs. Lemon returned home to find Mr. Lemon seated at the kitchen table, reading pornography and smoking a cigarette.

"Welcome to my mid-life crisis," he said. "How was the expedition?"

"Wonderful," she said. "I made many new and fascinating discoveries that will no doubt alter the course of human history quite significantly."

"That is excellent."

Mrs. Lemon sat down across from her husband and poured herself a cup of tea.

"You are smoking a cigarette," she observed.

"Yes."

"I hear they are very dangerous."

"That is true. They are quite forbidden to children and invalids."

He tore a page from his magazine and passed it across the table for his wife to look at. It was a picture of a naked lady.

"She is lovely," said Mrs. Lemon, "but, as usual, I fail to understand the nature of the scandalous."

"Do not worry," he said.

She sighed. "I fear I shall never be perverted."

Mr. Lemon grew bored with his cigarette and lit another.

"I am enjoying this crisis. It is a fine crisis."

"I am glad."

Mr. Lemon looked at Mrs. Lemon's hands adoringly.

"Your fingernails are encrusted with dirt and a great many secrets."

She smiled.

The sun had risen much earlier than Mr. and Mrs. Lemon had anticipated.

"How curious . . . ," said Mr. Lemon. He yawned. "I am finding that lately there is not enough night for my liking."

Mrs. Lemon sat up and began swallowing pills. She drank from the glass of water on her night table.

"It is my birthday," she said. "You must give me presents."

Mr. Lemon rolled over to face her. He sighed deeply and tragically.

"I know that it is your birthday. Happy Birthday."

"Thank you."

"I thought very deeply and with great concentration on the matter of what to give you on this day. I am indeed very glad that you were born, and was quite enthusiastic about celebrating the anniversary of the event, yet the perfect gift continued to elude me."

"Did you go to the shopping mall?" she asked.

"Yes. It was terrifying."

She nodded.

"As I walked home, I entertained many visions of gifts for you: Expensive wines that would stain your lips exotic colours, exquisite gowns to wear dancing in moonlight, flowers that would trigger memories of beautiful days, an amulet you might one day throw into the sea in a fit of romanticism . . . but I decided on none of these things."

Mrs. Lemon rolled onto her stomach and regarded him pleasantly, her chin cupped in her hands.

Mr. Lemon reached under the bed and handed her a box. She opened it to find a small yellow bird. It sang a tiny song, which they strained to hear. The bird looked at Mrs. Lemon and blinked. It briefly skipped across their bedsheets before flying through the open window.

"Thank you," said Mrs. Lemon. "I have never seen anything so perfect."

AVNER MANDELMAN

Cuckoo

My cousin Yochanan, who lost an eye in the Six Day War, left Israel in 1968, soon after, and went to America to make money. He stayed on Wall Street twenty-two years, working, as they say, like a donkey, and so never had time to get married. Or maybe he didn't want to; because though he had lots of offers, including a beauty queen (Miss New Jersey, 1987), and two El Al stewardesses, he was afraid they were all after his money. Which maybe was true, because in the meantime he had become a partner at Loewenstein Brothers, and was worth maybe four or five million dollars, plus his partnership interest. Finally in 1990, on a visit to Israel to see his mother (that's my father's sister Rivka), he also dropped in on my father in his tailor shop on Nachalat Binyamin Street, to talk, and to make a new suit (cheaper than Brooks Brothers), and there he met Pnina Chelnov, the daughter of Sarah Chelnov, the "1956 Nightingale" who had sung the famous "Nights of Blood," and who now gave her skirts to my father to be taken out or in, depending on her diet.

Now, Sarah's daughter Pnina was only twenty-four years old, sixteen years younger than Yochanan, and she had already been married once (for a year), to a Yemenite from Kerem ha-Teimanim named Yig'al Z'ruya, who had divorced her because she couldn't have children. Pnina herself was half Yemenite –

her mother, Sarah, was born in San'a, but had married Gavriel
Chelnov, the comic actor, and had one child – Pnina, who, like
many children of mixed marriages, was a beauty, with fair skin
and tight curly hair, and with the rollicking walk of a Yemenite,
but the legs of an Ashkenazi – everyone looked at her as she
walked down the street, or came into the grocery store to buy
bread, or eggs. So from here to there, Yochanan, who liked pretty
girls – though not to get married with – forgot about the suit and
took Pnina to lunch at Kerem ha-Teimanim, of all places, and
there, Pnina's ex-husband, who was a small-time criminal
(diamond burglaries), saw them eating humus together from
one plate and got jealous – though what did he have to get jealous
about? He and Pnina were divorced four years already! So he
slapped her on the face right at the table, before everybody.

From what I learned later, two policemen were also in the
restaurant (having Turkish coffee), one from the anti-terror
squad, the other from police-intelligence, but neither of them
did anything, because why get tangled up in something not your
business, and with a Yemenite, too? But Yochanan, who in the
army had been with the paratroopers (as an officer, though only
at the supply warehouse, in Sarafand), got up, and immediately
punched the ex-husband two times, once in the stomach, the
other in the face, and broke his (the Yemenite's) nose.

Now, although the restaurant (Tziyon's, on the corner of
Malkiel Street and Even-Chen) was full of Yemenites, from complete astonishment nobody did anything to Yochanan – later it
came out that Pnina had said to someone that he (Yochanan) was
a friend of Sammy Aboutboul, a Moroccan from the ha-Tikva
neighbourhood, who the year before had emigrated to America
to start a small mafia in Brooklyn; or maybe it's a tall tale, who
knows. But the result was that Yochanan and Pnina finished
their humus (with Pnina holding a cold Tempo bottle to her
cheek), and right after, she went with him to his suite at the Dan
Hotel, and the following week Yochanan told my father (who,

ever since Yochanan's own father had died in '56 in the Kadesh campaign, was like a father to him), that he, Yochanan, was getting married.

"To whom?" asked my father, who already guessed, but hoped it wasn't true.

"To her," Yochanan said, "Pnina Chelnov, that I met through you, here."

My father later said he felt a cold hand on his heart, because, to make a *shiduch*, a match, is a *mitzvah*. But this? What's the point for Jews to get married? Only, begging your pardon, to go to bed? For this you don't need a ring. For this, begging your pardon again, even *shiksas* are good, of which there are plenty in America. Jews get married to procreate, that's what for, like it says in the book of Genesis. But with Pnina a barren woman, and after a Yemenite, too (who most of them can make children even when they are eighty), why put a healthy head into a sick bed, as they say?

But Yochanan did not want to hear anything. "In my age," he said, "when I finally found love, I will marry her, no matter what anybody says."

"Yochanan," my father told him, "listen to me. With your money, you can marry a Rabbi's daughter, even, to be a good Jewish wife to you, and make you five children, ten, even. What do you need this one for?"

But, as they say, when a mule has made up his mind, nothing helps. So nothing helped here either, and after maybe two weeks, in which Yochanan also met Pnina's family (her mother Sarah, and two uncles in Hadera), he left for America, and after another week he sent her an El Al ticket (first class), and the next month they got married in the biggest synagogue on the upper West Side, right next to his co-op apartment.

So that's how it began. For the next two years they lived there, in New York, and also in Florida, where Yochanan had a little sailboat, and a condo, and also every year they came to

Israel to visit, and to see the family: from Pnina's side, her mother, and from Yochanan's side, us. (His mother had died right after the marriage.)

Pnina in the meantime had begun working in El Al's New York office, where Yochanan's chauffeur used to bring her every morning, after he drove Yochanan to work, until she told him to stop, because no one at work talked to her. She just wanted to be like everyone else.

Now if you ask me, I think Pnina was a good girl, and everything that happened was not her fault, both then, and later. Sometimes, like they say, God plays jokes and people suffer. And who does he like to play jokes on, most? Exactly. The Jews.

So, like I said before, the only problem of Pnina was she couldn't have children. Everything else, a husband, money, work, vacations, she had. Only no children. Not that she and Yochanan didn't try. They travelled everywhere, to the Caribbean, Paris, Gstaad, who knows where else, for the atmosphere, and maybe the air and the water, maybe something would help them relax. But nothing helped. Also, every year when they came to Israel, on Passover (usually they came to us, to the seder), they also went to doctors, first in Ichilov and Hadassah hospitals, then private, but the doctors could do nothing. There was nothing wrong with either Yochanan or Pnina, they said. Just no children.

So after a while Pnina began to keep a kosher kitchen in their New York apartment, just in case, and go to synagogue, and visit holy rabbis to get a blessing, or an amulet – I heard once that she had made Yochanan give maybe ten thousand dollars (some say a hundred thousand) to the Boyberisher Rebbe's charity, for a special amulet (a piece of paper with letters from the Kabbalah, and a clove of garlic and a coin inside). But again nothing helped. So then they began to talk about adopting, but of this also nothing came, because who knows who were the baby's parents? Maybe they were unmarried Jews, so he's a bastard? This can never be erased, to the tenth generation.

So finally finally, on one of the visits to Israel, a famous doctor in Hadassah found what was wrong with Pnina: her eggs were no good. Broken, or something. So no matter what, she would not be able to have children, amulets or no.

The very next day, Pnina came to my father's tailor shop and asked my father to go tell Yochanan she was offering him a *get*, so he, Yochanan, could at least get married with someone who could give him children.

My father did not want to give this message, because, first, in the meantime, barren or not barren, he had begun to like Pnina – because what was her fault if God decided to play such a cruel trick on her? And second, because while making a match is a *mitzvah*, making a divorce is a sin. So not only did he make such a bad mistake introducing Yochanan to this poor barren woman, he would now also be the messenger for the divorce? So he told Pnina, why don't you wait, maybe God will take pity on you? But she had made up her mind, and said, no, go tell him, so finally my father did.

But, like you guessed, Yochanan did not want to hear from a *get*. Some evil tongues said it would have cost him too much money, because to get divorced in New York is not like to get divorced in Tel Aviv. You are lucky if the wife leaves you a little shirt on your back. But I don't believe this. You only had to look at them, to see this was not a question of money, but real love for children. So again they talked about adoption, and my father said maybe he could ask from his friends on Lillienblum Street, that bought and sold gold, and marks, and dollars, to find where you can get a baby also, maybe in Be'er Sheva, or Magdi'el, where Russian immigrants, who had settled there, were usually willing to do things for money that no one else would; but Pnina said no. She did not want to take anyone else's baby, to build her happiness on the misery of others. A *get* was the only solution.

But then Pnina's mother, Sarah Chelnov, came out and said, I have another idea. I will do it for you.

"Do what?" said Pnina.

"I will carry your baby," Sarah said.

At first Pnina thought it was a bad joke. Because, let's face it, Sarah was then already forty years old (she had born Pnina when she was sixteen); and also, who had ever heard of such things? It was filth.

But then it came out Sarah hadn't meant she would, begging your pardon, go to bed with Yochanan. Just do it with a doctor, with a syringe. "Like an injection," she said.

At this both my father and mother said they didn't think it was possible, but Sarah said, they did it with cattle all the time.

"We are not cattle," my father said. "We are Zussmans."

Pnina, too, didn't want to hear from this. But after a while, little by little, it came out maybe it wasn't such a bad solution, because Sarah (who had just then begun recording again) had some free time, and was also not going out with anyone, and still had not, begging your pardon again, dried up as a woman. So, the following week, they all went to the lawyer Ya'acov Gelber, and wrote a contract (which Yochanan insisted on). Then the very next day they went, together with my father and mother, to Hadassah hospital, where Dr. Nissan Rivkin the gynecologist (the brother of the famous Pesach Rivkin, who wrote the articles about cancer), did what they asked.

Then Yochanan and Pnina went back to America, and waited.

This was the end of 1991, and the stock market was going crazy, so Yochanan busied himself with this, while Pnina did nothing but call her mother, to check, every day. But somehow the injection didn't catch, so after two months, Yochanan left the stock market and he and Pnina came back; and once again, they did it with Pnina's mother, and with Dr. Rivkin; and this time they waited in Tel Aviv, in the Dan Hotel, for the result; but once more it didn't catch. So again, they did it with Dr. Rivkin, and went to America to wait – it went like this for six more months, with no results, and they almost despaired, until Pnina said, "Maybe you just have to do it the way it should be done."

At first Yochanan thought she was joking, but she wasn't. So, to cut a long story, it also came out she had already talked to her mother, and she (her mother) already agreed, but she (her mother) wasn't sure if Yochanan would. Not because she, Sarah, was ugly (she wasn't), but because in the meantime, he, Yochanan, had become religious in America, and an adherent of the Boyberisher Rebbe, to whose court he was going every Saturday to partake of the Rebbe's table, and to pray, because of Pnina.

So, to cut it even shorter, Yochanan decided to put all this question before the Boyberisher Rebbe himself.

Now, normally, to get to see the Boyberisher for even a minute, is a miracle. Because, as is well known, from even one word of his mouth, the Heavens open. But with Yochanan, who for two years already was coming to the Rebbe's table, and was also giving in secret to the Boyberisher orphanage, there happened a special exception, and he got to see the Rebbe for a whole half-hour. Almost like Rabin, or Peres, when they come to New York. So of course evil tongues began to wag, and said the Rebbe did it because he, Yochanan, gave money, and maybe he also would give more; but this is not true, because some Jews much richer (like the Bronskys, or the Loewensteins) never got to see the Rebbe even for five minutes.

Anyway, no one knows what the Rebbe and Yochanan talked about, but the result was that Yochanan gave Pnina a *get*, written specially by the Boyberisher himself, then flew to Israel, where he went to see her mother. What they did nobody knows, because maybe they again went to Dr. Rivkin? Who can say for sure that they didn't? But the outcome was, that Sarah became pregnant, and nine months later she gave birth to two boys; and Yochanan and Pnina, who got married again, adopted them. Then Yochanan and Pnina and the two boys all came to live in Tel Aviv (on Maz'eh Street), where Lowenstein Brothers had just opened a branch for investment in Israeli high tech, and Yochanan was the partner in charge.

Now if you think that this is the end of the story, you are mistaken. Because the following year, right after Sarah Chelnov's new record came out (with 1956 songs, accompanied by a flute and a rababeh), Pnina's mother went cuckoo. At first no one realized this (because she only stopped cleaning her apartment, and washing the dishes), until she began to scream in the night that her happiness had arrived, but she gave it up. The neighbours asked her to stop shouting; then, when this didn't help, they called Pnina and Yochanan.

At first Yochanan and Pnina thought, this was because she had given up the babies. So they came often, with the boys, so Sarah could play with them, more like a mother than a grandmother (even though, as you can imagine, Pnina didn't like this), but soon it became obvious that who Sarah was after was not the boys, but Yochanan.

This was 1992, and Yochanan was forty-two years old, only one year older than Sarah, and looked good because he also did exercises (like running every morning on the Gordon beach, or lifting weights), and even if he had only one eye, he didn't put glass in it, only covered it up with a black patch, like Moshe Dayan, who, as everyone knew, was once Sarah's boyfriend. So, what can I say, Yochanan and Pnina just took the kids back to Maz'eh Street, and stopped coming; but then Sarah, who was not cuckoo enough to be put in the Bat Yam asylum (where there's never enough room), started coming to ring their doorbell in Maz'eh, or write letters to Yochanan and slip it under the door, or even cook humus (for Yochanan), and leave it on the doormat, in a pot, again with notes.

Finally Pnina couldn't take this any more, and she made Yochanan take her back to New York, with the children. And right after, her mother one night began to scream and sing so loud that finally the neighbours called an ambulance, and because Bat Yam was full, she was taken to Beit Tzedek Hospital, in Jerusalem, where someone who had once heard her sing in '56 was now a doctor; then for a while no one knew anything else.

This was already 1993, and the stock market was not so crazy any more, so Yochanan had some time on his hands. So again he began to go to the Boyberisher court, and from here to there, he became one of the helpers of Rabbi Shlomo Tzirelsohn, the Boyberisher minister of finance, so to speak. This job he, Yochanan, of course did for free, for the *mitzvah*; but free or not, little by little he began to give more time to the Rebbe, and less to Loewenstein Brothers. He also began to grow his sidelocks, and wear the black clothes of the Boyberisher Chassidim; and Pnina, even though she was keeping a kosher kitchen, and everything, did not like this very much. Because, let's face it, now that she had the boys, what did she need to be so religious for? Also, don't forget, she was only twenty-nine, maybe, so did she want to bury herself in the kitchen doing kosher? No. She wanted to go see shows on Broadway, maybe a concert, and movies. But now Yochanan did not have the time, or the will, to go. So from here to there, no one knows how it happened, Pnina one day met someone, in Brooklyn, and who do you think it was? No, not her ex-husband the Yemenite, but Sammy Aboutboul, who did not open a mafia after all, and was only moving furniture, with a truck. So from here to there, they started talking, about Tel Aviv, and soccer games (which Pnina used to go to, before she met Yochanan), then they sat down to have falafel (on Seventh Avenue and Eighty-Third), and finally Sammy asked if he could call her again, and she said, Okay, but only to talk.

And that's how it started. After a while, when Yochanan was spending even more time at the Boyberisher court (he no longer worked for Lowenstein Brothers – but he had enough money so he didn't have to), and Pnina said she was going out shopping (by that time they already had a nanny, from the Phillipines) – she really went out to see Sammy.

After maybe six months of this, it all came out, because someone who had seen Pnina with Sammy, in a movie, sent a letter – not to Yochanan, but to Rabbi Shlomo Tzirelsohn, for whom Yochanan was now working, for free, at the Boyberisher court; and in the letter, the evil tongues pretended they only had Yochanan's welfare at heart (else how could they allow themselves to write such a thing?) and asked Rabbi Tzirelsohn to give Yochanan some time off, so he could take care of his young wife, to prevent her from committing sin.

Because the Boyberisher was sick then, Rabbi Tzirelsohn couldn't ask his advice, so on his own idea he showed the letter to Yochanan. And when Yochanan read this, he took off his *kapota*, and his hat, and took a cab straight home. There he slapped Pnina like she had never been slapped before, and then he went back to Brooklyn to see Sammy Aboutboul. And there, even though Sammy was maybe thirty-six, and Yochanan, eight years older, and Sammy was lifting pianos and sofas and tables every day, and Yochanan, just doing calculations, he, Yochanan, beat Sammy up so bad that the neighbours had to call the police, and the police took him, Yochanan, to jail.

Now, listen to this: when Yochanan got out (due to special intercession on the part of the Rebbe, who in the meantime had gotten well), he saw that Pnina was not home – (later it came out she had gone to see Sammy, at the hospital) – and the children she left with the nanny. So without saying anything, Yochanan took the children, packed two suitcases, and called a cab to the airport. But there, instead of buying regular air tickets, he went to the private jet lounge, and asked the Lowenstein Brothers' pilot (the firm had two jets, both Astras, made in Israel) to take him and the children special to Israel. (As an ex-partner, he could use the plane, but he had to pay for it.)

When Pnina came back, and saw that the children were gone, she immediately called the police, and they alerted the airport, to look for a man with two children, going to Israel. But, like I said, Yochanan took the private jet of his old firm, so the very next day he landed in Lod, where no one knew of anything, so they let him in.

And where do you think he went? You are right, straight to the apartment of Sarah Chelnov, Pnina's mother.

Now, I already said that, right after Pnina and Yochanan had left, because Sarah Chelnov had gone crazy, she was taken to

Beit Tzedek hospital in Jerusalem. But after maybe two weeks there, she got well enough to be let out. But instead of returning to Tel Aviv immediately, she went first to Me'a She'arim, which is the most orthodox neighbourhood in Jerusalem, and went to see Rabbi Ury Blisker, who in those days was the first rabbi everyone who wanted to become religious went to. To no surprise, Rabbi Blisker told her to start keeping a kosher kitchen, and to go to synagogue, and to give to charity, but also to go back to Tel Aviv, not to stay in Jerusalem. When she asked if she should also continue to sing, and make records, he said yes, but also to make records of songs from the bible.

So what can I tell you? You probably know the rest. Sarah Chelnov then made a record (in November, 1994) of the "Song of Songs," together with a choir of simple Yemenites from the street, all kinds of verses, with melodies by Ne'omi Sharf, Nechemia Malchin, the Chamdi brothers, and others; and she sold maybe fifty thousand copies of this, which in Israel is unheard of. And from this money, she gave half to *yeshivot*, and to orphanages in Bnei Brak and in Jerusalem. So people bought even more records; and even religious people, who never listen to music, they bought also. So to make a long story really short, Sarah Chelnov became again a success, like she was once in 1956, and also became happy again, with synagogue, and prayer, and singing.

The only thing she didn't want to do, was get married with any one of the widowers or the divorced rabbis that Ury Blisker kept sending her (because it is a sin for a person to be alone, if he can make a Jewish family, and it's a *mitzvah* to make a *shiduch*, a match). But other than that, and the fact she no longer talked to her daughter, or her children, it was not the worst.

So it was then (this was January, 1995) that Yochanan came to her apartment, with the two children, straight from the airport.

What happened right after, I don't know exactly. My father said that, at first, Sarah Chelnov said, don't stay here, it'll be a sin; you are married to someone else. But Yochanan said, I'll sleep in the other room, but I stay here, because the children should be with their family, not strangers. So finally she agreed. But my mother, who says she heard this from Sarah's own grocer, insists that at the beginning Yochanan and the children did not even come to Sarah's apartment, but went instead to Hotel Z'vulun, which is the place all the orthodox Jews go to, two blocks from the Dan Hotel; and only after two weeks, when Yochanan finally got the *get* (he received it from the bet din, the rabbinical court, of the Chabadniks in Bnei Brak, saying he had a rebel wife), did he finally go to live with Sarah, together with the children.

But if you listen to the evil tongues (especially in *Ha'Olam ha-Zeh* magazine, where the gossip column is full of stories), this wasn't at all how it happened, because (that's what some of the stories say), it was Pnina who had left Yochanan, and only after she had discovered he was secretly corresponding with her mother, and promising to come see her, Sarah, soon. If you ask me, I don't know what's true. What I know is, after three days Pnina arrived from New York to Tel Aviv, and immediately hired the best lawyer, David Kupershnit (who was once assistant to the Minister of Justice), and sued Yochanan for custody of the children.

Now this really started the evil tongues going. Because, can you imagine? First there was the chance that Yochanans' talk with the Boyberisher would come up in court, and he would have to tell everything about the advice he got. Then, of course, out would come the answer if he and Sarah did do it like a husband and wife, or not; which nobody knew. And also would come out the part about Pnina and Sammy – who, after a little while, it came out did start a little mafia, and the moving business was only a cover. And if this was not enough, Pnina just then became pregnant, from Sammy, so she claimed she could provide the boys as good a home as Yochanan and her mother could.

What can I tell you? All this was so good and juicy, that for a whole month, even though Rabin was just then negotiating with the religious parties to go into the coalition, no one in Tel Aviv (also in other big cities) was talking of anything else. There was even a little fight among the judges, about who would sit on the case. Finally Judge Sorokin, who was about to retire, got it, and he began hearing evidence in March 1995 in the new court-room in Ramat Gan (the old family court, on Aliya Street, had just closed, in 1993).

Then everything stopped. Because, in the blood test, which they had to do, for the boys, it came out they were not Yochanan's at all. Can you imagine? At first, the lawyers did not know what to do, until Judge Sorokin (who did not get to be Chief Judge of the Appellate Court of the Dan District for nothing) said he wanted a blood test of everyone in the courtroom who came to watch. For this he was ridiculed for maybe a week, in all the newspapers; until it came out that the blood type that was the same as the boys was that of Pnina's ex-husband, the Yemenite, Yig'al Z'ruya. But because blood type by itself doesn't mean much, the judge also ordered this new DNA test for the ex-husband, and the entire trial stopped, for ten days, until the answer came back from the FBI lab in Cincinnati, that no question, Pnina's ex-husband, Yig'al Z'ruya, was the boys' father.

Now this became worse and worse. Because, just think of it, when did Sarah have time to meet him? Or did she maybe go to ask him in secret to fill the syringe, instead of Yochanan? Why? Besides, why would he? Then, finally, when they began to question Sarah, it came out that she did meet this Yig'al Z'ruyah in the Carmel market, after maybe the third or fourth injection, from Yochanan, and later also once in the Yemenite choir for her record, so maybe something happened, but she did not remember.

Now, when this came out, that the boys were really Pnina's ex-husband's, it really got complicated, because Yig'al Z'ruya then also got himself a lawyer (Amnon Braverman, who last month was indicted for bribing a government minister), and said he, too, wanted custody. And because he, also, in the mean-time had remarried, and had two children already (twins), and since he hadn't been in jail for already two and half years, he too, he said, could provide a good home for the boys.

Now, during all this, Yochanan and Sarah went on living together, but it was no longer peaceful. Whether it was because of what came out about Pnina's ex-husband, and Sarah, or whether because Pnina and her mother were now fighting over both Yochanan and the boys, who knows. Probably everything together.

But what really threw everything for a loop, was that, with all the blood tests being done, and the DNA tests, and everything, Pnina, who was now pregnant in the seventh month, decided to do a blood test also. And who do you think she found out was the father of her child? You are right. Yochanan. It came out that two months before she left him, in New York, they had once tried to make up (because the Boyberisher told them), and this was the result. So is God playing sick jokes on people, or what? I don't want to answer this, but if you want to, go ahead.

And how did this all finish?

At the end, Judge Sorokin did something that made just about everybody mad at him: he stopped the trial, and took everyone into chambers, and put fifteen policemen around the court, at every window, so no one could peek in, or listen, and for seven hours he and all the litigants tried to come to some kind of arrangement.

But what it was, nobody knows. The only thing known is that maybe three, four times a year, Sarah Chelnov (who in the meantime had married Sammy Aboutboul, who is now her manager) and her new baby fly to Florida from Tel Aviv, and also Yig'al Z'ruya and his new wife, and their children, and they all spend maybe a week with Yochanan and Pnina, and the three boys; and some of the children sometimes stay there, or sometimes they stay in Tel Aviv, with us. My father also was invited once to go to Florida, but he said he can't go, because, first, at his age (seventy-three) he doesn't know if he should fly in airplanes for the first time, he could come back in a coffin. And, second, if by mistake he makes another cuckoo *shiduch* like this one it'll be even worse, why help God mock us again? When God plays a joke on us Jews, he says, the only thing to do is take care of the children hurt by Him and refuse to laugh; because unfortunately it is not permissible to play a joke on Him right back.

ELYSE FRIEDMAN

Truth

They were to meet at Starbucks at five o'clock. At five-thirteen, Leslie drained her small black decaf and checked her watch. Just then, Martin entered and scanned the faces in the café. He advanced toward her.

"Leslie?"

"Hi."

"Sorry I'm late. Have you been here long?"

"Yes," she said, "over twenty minutes. But I'm always a bit early."

"I'm usually late," he said, taking a seat. "I wonder if that's the first sign that we're not going to get along."

"I don't know," she said. "Do you want something, a coffee?"

He glanced at the menu above the counter. "I'm too cheap to pay more than a buck for a cup of coffee. Besides, I'm already buzzing. Just had two cups with another prospective partner at the doughnut shop around the corner."

"Oh," she said, frowning. "How did it go?"

"Not well. When we spoke on the phone, she neglected to mention the fact that she has kids. Three of them. Personally, I don't care for children. Especially when there's more than one."

"I'm not wild about them either. My sister has two. They're always so filthy, you know?"

"I suppose, but that doesn't really bother me. What I object to is the way they divert all the attention to themselves. They're like little black holes, sucking up attention like light particles. You can't escape it. Even I fall for it. When I'm in a room with a kid, I find myself watching the kid, fake-chuckling at the kid's ostensibly cute antics, commenting on them. . . . It's like when there's a TV on in a bar; you don't want to look at it, but it keeps sucking you back in. Doesn't matter what's on – infomercials, a curling match – it just sucks you right in, you know?"

"Hmm," she mused. "I think you might have psychological problems that are incompatible with my own."

He smiled and fished a package of gum from his jacket. He offered her a piece.

"Does my breath smell?" she asked.

"I can't tell from here," he said. "I was concerned about mine, actually." He popped one shiny white tablet and slid the pack toward her.

"I'm okay," she said, pushing it back across the table.

"So," he said, pocketing the gum, "you're fatter than I thought you would be. I mean, not repulsively so. I can deal with your type and level of fatness; it's just not what I expected. You look thinner in your photo."

"I'm pretty normal from the waist up. It's my legs and ass that are fat. I have a lot of cellulite on my ass."

"You should post a photo that includes your bottom half."

"I know, I've thought about that. But I'm afraid I'll scare people off. This way, I can meet someone in person and, you know, maybe there'll be chemistry there, maybe they'll find me so charming and intelligent that they won't mind the extra bit of weight."

"I guess that makes sense. You have a pretty face."

"Yes, I know. Thank you."

"But I don't find you particularly charming or intelligent."

"But we've only just met."

"That's true."

A woman in a pink sweatsuit sat down at a nearby table. She had a baby in a corduroy papoose strapped to her chest. Martin's eyes fixed on the gurgling infant.

"You actually look a lot better than you do in your photo," said Leslie, following his gaze. "And while it concerns me that such a good-looking man is single – presumably, you have some profound and fundamental character flaws – I am physically attracted to you, and am prepared to set aside my initial reservations."

The baby jammed a fist into its eye and began to yell. Leslie smiled sympathetically at its mother.

"Listen," said Martin, "do you want to get out of here? Grab a drink or something?"

It was hot outside. The streets were crowded with Saturday people. Martin walked quickly and purposefully, passing several upscale watering holes.

"Look," said Leslie when they paused at a red light, "I wear high heels only when I don't have to stand for too long or walk anywhere. My feet hurt and I'd like to stop in there for a drink." She gestured to a hotel across the street.

"Hotel bars are notoriously expensive," said Martin. "There's a pub just a few blocks down from here. They serve cheap draft and it's close to my apartment. Even if we took a cab, it would be cheaper than going to that hotel. But I think we should walk it, since I don't know you well enough to share your pain or even care about your discomfort."

"You're pissing me off," said Leslie, "but I have a wedding to attend in three weeks and I'm afraid of what my so-called friends will think and say about me if I show up to another major event without a date."

The light turned green. They proceeded to the pub.

Leslie ordered a martini, dry, with olives. Martin ordered a draft beer.

"This isn't so bad, is it?" said Martin, dabbing the sweat from his forehead and settling back in his chair.

"The carpet smells like wet gerbils, the air is choked with smoke, the exposed midriff of the waitress makes me feel dumpy and inadequate, and this martini has far too much vermouth in it."

"It's a pub. You should order beer."

"Beer makes me fart. Also, I'm well on my way to becoming a bona fide alcoholic, and liquor, as they say, is quicker."

"You know, I've never been addicted to anything," said Martin. "Nothing, nada. And I find it difficult to sympathize with substance abusers – whether that substance is Häagen-Dazs or heroin. Having said that, I tend to be more forgiving of men who have problems with the bottle. In certain cases, I even view it as macho and stylish – a kind of Bukowski bravado, you know? But with women it strikes me as nothing more than intolerable weakness."

"I just had this image," said Leslie, "of taking the little plastic sword from my cocktail and plunging it into your larynx." She laughed and swallowed the last of her drink with a flourish.

"I have to say, the fact that you're a boozehound pretty much puts me off for anything long-term, but makes me wonder if I'll be able to take you home tonight and have insincere sex with you once you're sloppy drunk."

"It's entirely possible," said Leslie. Martin waved down the waitress and ordered another half-pint. Leslie ordered a double gin on the rocks with a twist.

"Thanks a lot, Jan," said Martin when the waitress brought their order. She faux-smiled and moved off. They sipped their drinks.

"So," said Martin.

"So," said Leslie.

"You're a talent agent."

"Yes," she said. "It's not very interesting and I don't particularly enjoy it. And if you're bringing this up because you happen to be a closet actor, or know someone who's trying to break into the business, I'm going to guzzle this as fast as I can and then bolt."

"I'm not and I don't."

"Good."

"I'm just trying to make conversation and discover, in a roundabout fashion, how successful you are and perhaps even how much money you earn."

"I earn quite a lot of money. How successful I am depends on how one defines success."

"Well, the money part is a good start. Do you have any movie stars on your roster?"

"No."

"TV?"

"No. Not unless you count commercials. Almost all of my commissions come from commercials and voice-overs. You know Microbe Man?"

"Of course. The germ-fighting super-hero."

"I rep him, for example."

"Not terribly glam."

"No."

"You mentioned that your younger sister is in the biz?"

"She's a development exec at CBS. Very powerful and important. I'm quite proud of her, but also intensely jealous. I would like her to fail."

"She has kids, right?"

Leslie nodded. "And a wonderfully supportive husband who I happen to be hot for, and a gorgeous apartment and a palatial summer home. Oh yes, and a golden retriever, which I find kind of cliché."

"Already I'm more intrigued by your sis than I am by you," said Martin. "And if she didn't have rug rats, I'd probably start dating you just to get to her."

"She's in remission from breast cancer," said Leslie. "When she first told me she was ill – around seven years ago – all I could think of was whether or not I was genetically predisposed. Then I had this flash of her husband and me seeking solace in each other's arms after her death."

"Very nice."

"Later, when I learned that she wouldn't have to lose her perfect left breast, I felt tremendous relief, but also a tiny glimmer of indignation. I think I felt she would be easier to love without it." Leslie drained her drink and sighed. "Well, I guess I'll go home, put on *Blonde on Blonde*, turn out all the lights, and get shit-faced."

"Listen," said Martin, "my self-esteem will be temporarily boosted if I get you into bed tonight; and that waitress is making me kind of horny. Why don't we go to my place? I have booze. It'll be cheaper than ordering another round."

Leslie mulled it over. "Why not," she said. "I have masochistic inclinations and I'm feeling rather self-destructive."

"Then it's settled," said Martin, signaling for the bill.

Leslie paid the tab, and they left.

Martin lived in a recently constructed, loft-style condominium unit – large windows, hardwood veneer floors, useless ductwork painted white and suspended from the high ceilings for an industrial/artsy effect. It was a roomy suite, sparsely decorated with severe, monochromatic furniture.

"I would like to know at once," said Martin, tossing his keys into an ashtray by the door and dimming, ever so slightly, the halogen track lighting, "if you're as impressed as I feel you should be by my carefully coordinated, evidently upscale living space?"

"Mildly impressed," she said, "but mostly confused by the fact that you're clearly a cheap-ass, yet you own what I'm certain is a pricey, albeit shoddily built condo in a decent location."

"I don't own it," said Martin. "I rent it. I'm obsessed with status and the need to appear successful."

"That would explain the oversized Patek Philippe on your wrist."

"So you noticed?" Martin admired his own timepiece.

"Almost immediately," said Leslie.

"It's a fake," said Martin with a mirthless smile.

"So, in addition to being shallow, you're also a poser?"

"Somewhat of a poser," said Martin, "and a little shallow. But it's not as simple as that. I happen to be reacting to early childhood influences. I come from a large family – four brothers, three sisters. My parents were immigrants, dirt poor, and completely unsuccessful in their tenacious struggle to achieve even lower-middle-class respectability."

"Boo hoo," said Leslie. "Cry me a river."

"And now my half-baked dot-com business venture is stillborn, I'm up to my sternum in credit card debt, I had to give up my BMW, which was leased anyway, and my prospects for rewarding employment are rapidly fading."

"So too is my interest in you."

"Well," said Martin, "I think the cold-hearted lush needs a drink." He moved toward the open-concept kitchen area. "Make yourself comfortable."

"I'm not sure that's possible," said Leslie, perching on the edge of a moulded plywood bench. She watched him pour a half-tumbler of straight booze from a giant plastic bottle of no-name gin.

"Panty remover," said Martin, dropping two ice cubes into the drink. He stirred it with his finger, not bothering to turn his back.

"That's revolting," said Leslie. "If it weren't for the antibacterial properties of straight alcohol, I wouldn't dream of letting that pass my lips."

"You germ-phobic types really give me a pain," he said, handing her the glass.

"Aren't you having anything?"

"I wouldn't mind a beer, but I'm afraid I won't be able to get it up if I drink any more. Now then," he said, "would some music help to put you at ease and hasten our transition to the bedroom?"

"If it's the right music, probably."

"Why don't you pick something then?" He gestured to several CD towers beside the stereo. "I'm going to go take a piss and try to mask my chronic halitosis with a surreptitious tooth-brushing and repeated gargles of Listerine."

Leslie studied the titles on the racks. She was still looking them over when Martin returned from the bathroom.

"Do you like jazz?" he asked.

"I feel I should, but I don't."

"You're taking an inordinate amount of time to select something. Are you judging me by my discs?"

"Yes, I am," she said. "Most of your collection seems worthy but pretentious. You have all the important jazz –"

"Which I rarely listen to."

"And all the correct classical –"

"Which I never play."

"But your pop collection is varied and interesting and bears a lot of overlap with my own. And, most encouraging, you have more soul than I expected."

"How about this?" said Martin, pulling out *Sensuous Seventies Soul Grooves, Volume 3*.

"I love that series," said Leslie, "but isn't it a bit cliché, a bit heavy-handed for a middle-aged white guy in Sperry Topsiders to be playing such blatantly sexual African-American music on a first encounter such as this?"

"It's also cliché to lubricate with oil, but it gets the job done, doesn't it? And since there's nary a James Brown tune on this particular compilation, I believe it's within reason."

Moments later, Leslie was undulating, drink in hand, to the mellifluous sounds of Al Wilson singing "Show and Tell."

Martin watched her sip and sway, sway and sip with her eyes half-closed. "Aren't you drunk yet?" he asked.

"I'm just perfectly and beautifully tipsy," said Leslie. "And, provided you don't have herpes or any other disease that could be transmitted orally, I wouldn't mind at all if you kissed me now."

Martin took the glass from her hand and placed it on a speaker. Then he leaned in and found her lips, and kissed her lightly a couple of times. She drew him close and pushed her tongue deep into his mouth. After a few seconds, he pulled away slightly.

"I'm worried about my breath," he said.

"It ain't great," said Leslie. "And while it's a factor that would disturb me over time, I'm too turned on at the moment to give a rat's ass."

They smiled at one another and resumed smooching. Martin squeezed Leslie's left breast. "Sufficiently firm," he mumbled, "but difficult to tell with the bra on."

She moved her hand over his crotch, locating the hard-on. "I'm relieved to find that I'm making you horny," she said, and reached for the zipper in his pants.

"Let's go to the bedroom," he whispered.

"Wouldn't it be more spontaneous, more like an exciting Hollywood movie starring Glenn Close, if you took me right here on the floor?"

"Yes. But it would be infinitely more comfortable to take you in the bed."

"And the condoms are in there," she said, allowing herself to be led, by hand, into the bedroom. "Hey, nice sheet set, Martin."

"Thanks."

She ran her hand over the duvet cover. "Did a woman friend pick this out?"

"No, I did."

"You're not gay, are you?"

"I don't think so. I mean, I've never done it with a man. But occasionally when I'm masturbating or even having sex with a woman, I'll get this image of a good-looking guy stroking his large, naked penis."

"I can live with that," she said. "Um, before we get down to it, I should probably hit the bathroom. I'm prone to painful bladder infections, and my doctor told me I should urinate before and after sex."

"In there," he said, pointing.

"Be right back."

Martin fished out some condoms and placed a couple on the

bedside table for easy access. Then he quickly stripped off his clothes and slid under the duvet. He did a breath check and sniffed his pits. He waited. He waited some more. He heard the water running. He heard the toilet flush. He heard the water again. Eventually, Leslie reappeared.

"What took you so long?"

"I was snooping through your medicine chest. Then I checked my nipples to make sure there were no unsightly hairs sprouting around them. After that, I emptied my bladder, and passed gas while the toilet was flushing so you wouldn't hear me. Finally, I gave my vagina a little freshening sponge bath with some wet toilet paper. I dried myself on your hand towel."

"Strip," he said.

She took off her shoes and started unbuttoning her blouse. "I would feel more comfortable if you turned out the light."

"But I want to see what I'm getting."

"I'm too ashamed of my body to undress in these harshly lit conditions."

Martin switched off the bedside lamp. A bit of streetlight spilled in through the window, barely illuminating Leslie as she shed her clothes and slipped into bed.

"My eyes haven't adjusted to the light yet," said Martin, "but from what I could tell, you look pretty good."

"That's a relief."

"Now, I just have to worry about a) whether you'll deem my penis to be of sufficient length and girth, b) maintaining an erection while I struggle into a condom, c) premature ejaculation, and d) performing sensually and acrobatically enough for you to be pleasured to the point of orgasm thereby concluding that I'm good in bed."

"I hope you're circumcised," she said, ducking under the duvet. "Any STDs I should be aware of?" came muffled from beneath the covers.

"Scabies in college, but I've been clean and tested since then," said Martin. And she took him into her mouth. He flipped back the cover to watch her. After several heated moments he said, "Stop, or I'll shoot."

"Yes, officer," she said, slyly. "Whatever you say."

"Stop that too. I'm not into silly role-playing." He pulled her toward him, then pushed her onto her back. He kissed her mouth and her neck. He massaged and licked her breasts. She held his head in her hands. She made no sound. "Are you enjoying this?" he asked.

"Very much, but I'm preoccupied with how they look."

"They're a bit lopsided and not as big as I'd like, but they're reasonably firm and attractive."

She smiled and relaxed her grip on his skull. He kissed slowly down her belly, pausing just below the navel.

"Keep going," she said.

"I don't really want to; I don't like doing that. But I will, just to demonstrate that I'm a conscientious lover." He continued moving down.

"Mmm," she said. "You're not very skilled, but it feels good nonetheless."

"Enjoy it while you can. I only do it on first encounters." After about fifteen seconds, Martin sat up, reached for a condom, and tore open the packet. He rolled onto his back and slid it on. "Listen," he said, "I'm kind of pooped from my spinning class this morning – why don't you climb aboard?"

"Because I'm submissive, and I prefer to be on my back or my knees."

"Oh, all right." He got on top.

"Ow," she said, "you're on my hair."

"Sorry." He adjusted his position. "How's that?"

"That's nice. Mmm, that's *very* nice."

Slowly, they got into the rhythm of the thing. Leslie closed her eyes. She began to moan, softly at first, then not so softly.

"What are you thinking about?" he whispered.

"Tom Cruise," said Leslie.

"Me too," said Martin. And before long, with a grind and a whimper from Leslie, and a clenched-jaw growl from Martin, it was all over. He collapsed onto her, then rolled off with a sigh. He removed the condom carefully, tying it closed with a knot and examining it for defects. He placed it on the bedside table, crossed his hands over his belly, and closed his eyes. Leslie wiped the sweat from her face and pulled the duvet up over her body. *Sensuous Seventies Soul Grooves* came to what seemed an abrupt end, and all they could hear was faraway traffic and the sound of their own breathing.

"How do you feel?" asked Martin, his eyes still shut.

"Dejected," said Leslie.

"You came though?"

"No. I faked it."

"Oh." He turned onto his side, his back to her.

"Are you angry?"

"No. I'm disappointed. Ashamed. I can't seem to do anything right these days."

"I'm sorry," said Leslie. "I just wanted it to be good for you, so that you might want to see me again and repeat the experience."

"Why the hell would *you* want to?"

"Because it felt warm and good, because I crave physical human contact, because it's been over a year since I've had sex, because I'm tired of going for massages just to have another person's hands on my body." She exhaled deeply and stared at Martin's broad white back.

"I feel afraid," he said, quietly.

"Of what?"

"Failure. Poverty. Ridicule. Death."

"Yes," she said. "And disease. War. Loneliness. Aging."

The mournful howl of a distant siren dopplered through the air.

They reached for one another in the dark room.

ROSARIA CAMPBELL

Reaching

J ust before I go to sleep at night is when it creeps up on me so I count toenails then. Two per hind foot, two hind feet per pig, sixty pigs an hour, eight hours a day. Dianne says that's almost two thousand toenails a day and I'm not even forty yet, so when things are really bad I try to add up how many in twenty years, until I retire. It's a little game I play with myself because I learned a long time ago that sometimes you can't keep it out, no matter how hard you try.

Sometimes, though, I see the moon. I'm driving just south of Saskatoon where the highway's rolling a little and it's warm enough to open the windows and you can smell spring in the air. In northern Saskatchewan spring smells like dry soil and there's little oil wells in the fields. There's no one else on that highway and every now and then the tires hit a rock or a pothole and I'm going to pick Dianne up. The wind feels so good that I reach out to her where she's breathing alongside me in the bed and I wrap my arms around her. I lay there like that and I think that a guy like me, who never even finished high school, is damned lucky to have a job at all when you think about it.

At exactly 7:20 the overhead rail jumps a little and then it starts moving and it doesn't stop until break at 9:40. I'm down the line a ways so I normally watch the spot on the wall in front of me and look busy until the first carcass comes by and I start pulling toenails off the hind feet with a stainless-steel hook. I drop them down into the gutter and someone else sweeps them up and that's about all there is to it unless there's a problem and we get a line stop, usually just enough time for me to rest my arm for a bit, stretch and wait. If it's long enough some of the guys horse around, make signs to each other about what they did on Friday night or about their girlfriends. We're in negotiations right now, so the line stops a lot.

Today the killfloor is short two people and the lead hand asks me to fill in for a dentist's appointment, scraping the inside of the legs where the brushes can't get at. I'm not crazy about it but the shop steward okays it so I go where they tell me to. I'm there when the line stops the first time and I lean forward, rest my head on the side of the pig in front of me. It's solid and I can feel the heat and moisture from the pigs and the concrete and I doze there like that, against the pig. And I dream too. I dream about the night I picked Chad up for the first time. I showered first and then washed my hands twice because I didn't want anything from the plant touching him. He was asleep in a blanket and I wasn't sure what I was supposed to do so I just smelled the top of his head, felt how soft the hair was there. Later the guys took me out and bought beer and cheap cigars and I got so drunk I ended up sleeping in the hallway outside the apartment. I made it in to work the next day but I could still smell him, even over all the other smells in here.

I'm still leaning on that pig when the line jumps, but I just shift my weight and go back to work. I can sleep standing on my feet if I need to, and I'm always ready when the line starts again.

Chad's seventeen now, and the two girls – Jennifer and Angie – are fifteen and thirteen. He's taller than me and he's a swimmer, good enough to make the provincial team if he tried out.

He'll be graduating from high school next year so I got him on at the plant this summer, filling in for vacation time. Dianne didn't like the idea much, and neither did I, but he needs the extra money for college and with the contract up at the plant now no one is sure what's going to happen. It's like gold to him because summer pay's not bad here and he's never worked at anything other than a paper route. He's shackling this week and it's a shitty job but he doesn't complain. The young guys like to show off their muscles down there in the pit and by now he's made it through five weeks, just past the point where they start to get cocky.

On his first day he rode in with me and he was so nervous he didn't even bother to turn on the radio, which is usually the first thing he does when he gets in the car. But when I asked him if he was all right he got pissed off with me and we didn't talk until we pulled off onto Marion. By then I could smell the rendering plant and recognize most of the cars around me, but it was all kind of new to him.

"Was Jimmy there when you started?" he asked, and I tried to remember what it was like to walk in there for the first time and have a dozen or more guys sizing you up, poking at your shoulder, trying you out.

"Yeah," I said. "Jimmy's kind of like the welcome wagon there." I was trying to make light of it, but he just turned away from me. "Jimmy's got a big mouth," he said, and when we drove through the front gates he was staring out the window and tapping his fingers on the dash, not saying anything at all. I knew it wasn't easy for him because he'd been a lot more sheltered than I'd ever been, and because I'd made it a point to keep it that way. I felt like I was breaking a promise to him and to me, but he only hesitated once. That was in the parking lot, when he saw four or five dozen cars there already, people moving in through the main doors in little groups. He stuck close to me and Jimmy and we gave him enough space so he didn't think he looked new, but inside the door I had to show him the window where he had to sign for his clock number. He snapped at me then, so Jimmy slapped him on the back.

"Couple of days and you'll be punching in with your eyes closed," he said to Chad. "Couple of years and they'll goldplate your timecard, like they did for me and your old man."

Of course everyone laughed at that. I watched Chad to see what he would do because this was like a hello and a little test rolled into one, and because there's a fine line on your first day between saying something back and being lippy. I could see he was tensed up but he didn't say anything and by the time we punched in and got our gear from the laundry everyone was back to Monday morning and Chad was in the middle of a couple dozen guys getting into their whites. I was watching them checking him out when the foreman came in with a clipboard and threw a freezer coat at him and took him off to start his first day. Jimmy was grinning at me like I had accomplished something, but I didn't see it that way. In my mind I was watching Chad follow the foreman into the coolers, and I was thinking that the difference between me and Chad was the difference between two months and eighteen years, and maybe that was why he never looked at me the whole time.

I try to stay clear of him at work and let him find his own way, and he does okay most of the time. The older guys don't like the summer help much, and Chad's already had a run in with Jimmy over work-to-rule. Jimmy's one of the oldest guys in the plant, here thirteen years already when I started. He's been shop steward more times than I can count and he's religious about work-to-rule, more so than anyone else here. He carries his union book around with him wherever he goes and listening to Jimmy talk sometimes is like reading that book, he knows it so well. Chad doesn't understand that and I guess that's my fault because I've never really explained to him about how things are done in here, about how you talk to people.

"You're crazy if you think I'm giving up the chance for time-and-a-half just because someone like you says I should," he said to Jimmy one day, because it's almost a tradition here for the summer help to try to get Jimmy's goat. It was kind of half-hearted, whole-earnest and Jimmy was going to grieve it, but the shop steward owed me a favour and I got him to talk to Jimmy until finally he calmed down.

"Keep your little college maggot the fuck away from me," he said, "or he'll find out what a fucking grievance is and so will you." I knew that's how Jimmy talks to everyone, but it still stung. Jimmy and me aren't great friends or anything but he's got his good points. When Dianne was sick after Jennifer was born and she needed some help around the house he got me a loan through the union, interest-free and no questions asked. And he always plays by the rules.

"You need people like Jimmy in a place like that," I told Chad that evening, "or there wouldn't be any difference between you and the pigs most days." Chad just shrugged so I tried to explain Jimmy to Chad, how he never really got back on his feet after his wife died, how the company screwed him out of his job because he was off two extra weeks watching her die and he had to come back in at the bottom when they wouldn't let him keep his seniority.

"When he came back into the plant he dug himself a hole and that's where he's spent every day since. He doesn't move a toe in that place unless he's got that book protecting him." Chad still didn't say anything so I left it at that because if I tried to tell him what to do or think it would strain things between us, and nothing in here is worth that to me.

Today at first coffee I sit by the window with a couple of the older guys and Chad sits across the cafeteria, between the sticker and the stunner. It goes without saying here that if you've been around for more than five years you get to choose your own seat, and this summer I'm glad for that rule because it means Chad can take his breaks on his own and neither one of us has to say why. The cafeteria is loud today and everyone is talking about the negotiations, mostly rumours and specula-tion. I've been here for eighteen years now, and I haven't seen or heard too much that's different during talks. The only thing that's different this year is that we're under new management and we're three weeks away from a vote and no one's heard a thing from the committee. I tell myself that it won't be that bad and smoke my cigarette, try to ignore everything around me. But I still hear little bits and pieces, even over the noise in the cafeteria and the forklift on the loading dock. The big rumour today is that there's going to be a buyout.

"You going to take it if it comes through, Paul?" Jimmy asks me. He looks bad today, and he's about the same colour as the concrete on the killfloor. My shoulder is stiff from the different motion of the scraping knife and when I turn around to answer him he says, "Or is Chad going to make enough money scabbing to support his old man?"

I'm ready to tell Jimmy to go to hell when I notice that his hand is shaking, even though he's supposed to have been off the booze for over a year. I know enough not to get into anything with Jimmy when he's hungover, and Chad's only got another three weeks so I just tell him I was hoping to stay on until the girls finish school and butt my smoke. The clock still has three minutes and twenty-four seconds left on it so I head for the washroom. The last thing I need today is to sit around listening to everyone getting pissed off.

I get back to the floor early and go to my regular spot and stand under the pigs for the last forty-seven seconds. While I'm standing there a little barn sparrow finds its way in through the shackling pit and gets lost in the carcasses until finally it pitches on a ham and starts picking at the skin. I watch him until the killfloor starts to come back and he flies off between the pigs' legs and disappears around a curve in the line. The pig jerks in front of me then so I pull my ear defenders down and pick up my hook, forget the gossip, and start reaching for toenails.

You're always reaching for something here. You spend your days reaching for pigs, reaching for knives, reaching for hoses. When

I first started I'd dream I was leaning out over the catwalk and then I'd feel for the edge and it wouldn't be there and I'd drop over into the gutter or the blood pit. I'd wake up on the edge of the bed with Dianne over on the other side and I'd go to the kitchen for a cigarette and stare out the window, wondering what would happen if I left. It usually came on after one of the guys had been by looking for me to go out, or after I'd seen Jimmy coming in to work hungover, talking about where he'd been the night before or the three days before. It wasn't that I didn't want to stay with her, just that I wanted to get away long enough to get the smell of pigs out of my nose.

I'd stay like that until dawn sometimes and then she'd come out into the kitchen with me, wanting to know what was up. She was getting big by then and it was something new for me, watching her grow like that.

"Sometimes even jail looks good compared to that place," I'd tell her, and she'd say to just hang on until something better came along, that we'd get by somehow, even if it meant less money. But when you didn't have good references there was never anything better, there was just the plant. And then it would always come up.

"I can go to work after the baby is born." And I know she would have, but I could always see her old man standing at the side of the squeeze chute, asking me how in the hell I thought I was going to support her. Dianne's father was a beef farmer, and it almost broke his heart the summer we ran off together because he had Dianne's life all planned out for her – college, marriage, kids, a job, half the farm eventually. But that all changed when I came along. I'd never finished high school and back then I couldn't even hold a job, had already been hauled up for a couple of small things like disturbing the peace, drunk and disorderly. I just ended up in Saskatoon one weekend and when I ran out of money I borrowed someone else's licence and drove dump trucks during the grain harvest. That's where I met

Dianne and why I stayed there for nearly a year, working at a scrapyard in Saskatoon until she finished school.

It nearly tore her to pieces to leave Saskatchewan, but we were both young and we thought we were going to see the world. "There's got to be more out there than dust and forty below and the ass end of a beef cow," she told me one night when we were coming home from the bars in Saskatoon, wondering how we could sneak her back into the house. That night I talked her into moving back to Winnipeg with me and we stayed with my brother Ray until she got pregnant. I needed work then, and Ray knew people at the plant so he got me a job in the holding barns and we moved into our own place.

I'd always get stubborn about her going to work. "Something'll come up," I'd tell her, and we'd have coffee then, with the sun coming up through the kitchen window. Sometimes we'd make time to go back to bed and I'd forget about Ray and Jimmy and whatever it was they still had and I'd clock in late. Those mornings I knew I wasn't going to leave and after Chad was born I went permanent, and I've been here ever since.

I stopped dreaming at night once I learned not to think about what I was doing during the day. After a year I could do almost anything they threw at me, and that's when I learned to sleep, to count, to stare, to wait. Anything other than think about what was in front of me all day long. Sometimes a whole morning would go by and I wouldn't be able to remember what I'd done on the line. I could remember thinking about what Dianne had smelled like on Saturday night, or about fishing at Lockport with her on Sunday, the first time I gave her my paycheque, the day I went permanent. Later it was teaching the girls to play catch or Chad how to swim or the day he told me he was going to college. "It's called AutoCAD," he said when he came home from school. "It's like drafting but it's all on computers." After that it was what the girls might end up doing and how much we'd need to put aside for them, what it would be like with just me and Dianne in the house someday.

Dianne told me last month that she's going back to school as soon as the girls are on their own. "Maybe I'll even finish something," she said. She's been taking a few courses a year for about five years now, and sometimes she finishes them and sometimes she doesn't. She wants to teach little kids, in preschool or kindergarten, because she's good with them and all her life she's volunteered at the school for things like field trips and museum visits. Now that the kids are older she's taking a computer course so she can follow what they're doing.

I'm pulling toenails and thinking about Dianne when I notice that the fans aren't keeping up with the heat from the pigs and that it's getting hard to breathe on the floor. I'm starting to see changes in the faces I can see because we're behind today and they're trying to speed things up so everyone is pissed off. There's something else too, but I'm not sure what it is so I go on hooking toenails until finally it comes around to me. I don't even see it at first, not until Jimmy points to the pig I'm working on. I turn the pig and there's a cartoon pinned to the ham, a picture of a great big boar leaning back on his hind legs with his balls dragging on the floor and the company name printed on his side. He's humping a half-dead old sow and on her front shoulder it just says "40% Cut." It's the first number we've seen since the negotiations began.

I try not to look at Jimmy because I know he's watching everyone's face while the cartoon works its way around the floor – I don't even need to turn around to see that. I keep on ripping toenails and calculating what it'll mean on my paycheque, even though I should know better, should know that it's probably just another rumour. But it's out there now and it'll stay there until we hear something different. I'm working out the weekly cut by the time the yelling starts down the line so I close my eyes and concentrate on Chad, try to think about how I'm going to explain this to him. Not the layoffs or the wage cut or the uncertainty, but how our future comes to us in a cartoon stuck to the side of a pig and how we've got to take it seriously and answer it. When I open my eyes again Jimmy is making signs for everyone to get ready for something, and I get ready too. I'm halfway through the second foot when someone hits the emergency stop for the line and the whole killfloor downs their tools, stands there under the pigs with their arms crossed until the line foreman comes in and gets it going again.

He doesn't ride home with me this evening. There's a note under the windshield wiper saying he's gone to shoot some pool, but I know it's because he doesn't want to have to talk about what's happening at the plant. I leave the parking lot without waiting to see what everyone is saying and I drive home in the afternoon breeze. It's the only time of the day that ever really feels like it's mine, and today I spend it thinking about Chad.

When Chad was eight he saw us on TV, trying to tip over a car. We were six weeks into a lockout on the first shift of the day and it wasn't even light yet. The pickets were set up just outside the main gates where they bring the trucks in and everyone was just standing around trying to keep warm, no one saying much any more. We heard something in the plant and saw the lights come on and we all turned around to check it out because we knew something was up. When Jimmy turned back to the parking lot he spotted the cars coming in through the side gates and the spotlights hit us just as we reached the first one. There were cops there too, but we held on and eventually the cars turned back. The cameras had what they wanted though, and while I was at an emergency meeting that night Chad was watching it on TV in the living room. By the time I got home he'd seen it three times, in the little commercials they run to let you know what's coming up in the news.

When I put him to bed that night he wanted to know why we had tried to tip over the car. They had shown a few shots of the plant in the background and then they zeroed in on a half dozen of us lined up on either side of the first car, rocking it and pounding on the roof with our fists. My hands were still shaking and my breathing felt too loud in his bedroom, so I waited for a few minutes before I answered him. I was listening to Dianne and Jennifer reading a book with Angie next door, trying to think of what to say to him. *"Ball. Wall. We all play ball upon a wall."* Angie was repeating the words after they said them and I could picture her tracing them with her fingers. It was one of those books we all knew by heart because Angie had made us read it so often. I told him it was because they were going to take our jobs but that wasn't enough because he'd seen the fucking shit and he was thinking about it. He wanted to know if the car had tipped over would anyone have been hurt so I told him that no one wanted to tip it over, just to stop it from going in. Dianne had explained to the kids what a lockout meant and why I couldn't go back to work. Everything except this. I asked him what they said on the news, but all he could remember was that car, and how mad everyone was.

"It could have tipped over," he said to me. "I saw it almost go over once." And maybe it could have, but I didn't tell Chad this. I didn't want to have to sit there in his bedroom and explain it to him, just like I didn't want to have to be tramping back and forth in front of that building every day like some kind of criminal.

"It'll probably all be over by next week," was all I said. I turned off the lamp then and sat on the bed with him until he fell asleep, listening to Dianne reading and counting up how many more contracts there would be before he finished school.

That same weekend Dianne went out and bought the kids a little plastic telescope, a book called *The Heavens*, and a map of the stars. Then she got some glow-in-the-dark paint and a pack of stencils and we spent every evening for three weeks teaching the kids about the stars, painting the sky on Chad's ceiling and learning the names of everything up there. Dianne did this to make sure the TV stayed off, because Chad had had nightmares three nights running. We took him into our room so I could get up with him and I thought that it would pass in a few nights, but Dianne was determined he'd have something to help him forget.

"He's not going to just forget about it," she said, "so maybe this will give him something to distract him."

And it did, too. He took to the stars like he'd been born out there. We'd all go out in the backyard in our winter coats, trying to find them on the map. The girls were too young to be much interested in it and I'd sit with them while Dianne and Chad stood off in the yard with little plastic flashlights, listening to them yelling out the names from the map. "I've got it," one of them would say, and then try to give directions to the other one. I don't think they ever found much more than the Big and Little Dippers, maybe a few planets. The most fun was when Dianne tried to find our signs up there, and I still remember our signs from those nights out there in the backyard. I'm a Pisces, Chad's an Aries, and Dianne and Angie are both Libras. Jennifer's a Taurus, the bull, and we all got a kick out of that because she was always breaking something at that age.

I remember one night Angie asked me what holds them up there and I didn't really have an answer for her so Chad came over to the deck and told her that it was gravity, the same thing that holds us on the earth and keeps us from flying off into space. Besides the book Dianne had bought he had taken another three or four out of the library, so he knew more about these things than I did. He was convinced he was going to be an astronaut that fall.

The lockout wasn't so bad in that way because I was able to spend some time with them and do some of the things I'd always heard Dianne talking about when I got home at night. Normally I was gone in the morning before they got up, working on the house or napping when they came home in the evenings. I was always off to the side, never right in their circle like Dianne was, so this was like stealing time for me. But it only lasted another couple of weeks, until I went back to work and everyone settled back into their own routines again. It was getting too cold anyway, and by that time Chad had settled down at night and the girls were getting bored with the stars.

But Chad kept that book in his room and read it every night, and he liked to sit in the living room and stare at things through the wrong end of the telescope while I caught the hockey game or the news. "I've got to make everything smaller," he'd say when he looked around the room. "When you make everything smaller it all fits better."

I got a bum shoulder the year I worked on the splitting saw and tonight Dianne rubs it while I watch the news on the TV in the bedroom. It's hot upstairs, even with the fan going, and she isn't saying much. I know what's bothering her, but I can't do anything about it so I tell her there's no real news today, that the same guys are still holed up in the same hotel, arguing over a couple of words or ten cents an hour, that the cartoon was just a joke. Her hands move slower on my shoulder, and then they stop. I ask her if she wants a back rub.

"No," she says. "I want to know how in the hell we're supposed to live on nine dollars an hour." I've got nothing to say to this, and she's not really asking me anyway. In the mirror behind the TV she's looking tired tonight. She only gets to talk about this after the kids are in bed and by then I'm usually sick of it so she's kind of outside of it all. But it still leaves her pretty tired.

"I'll have to go full-time if I can get it," she says then. "I don't see how we can do it otherwise." I can hear the disappointment in her voice and I watch her face in the mirror. She works a dozen or so hours a week in a drugstore and we talk for a while about her going to work full-time. She's okay with that. Whatever it takes, she's okay with it, but she wanted to take more courses this year, now that the kids are older.

"We can go into savings until I can get something else." I say this to the TV more than to her. After Chad was born her father started putting money into the bank every year for the kids and these last few years we've been matching it, for when they finish school. I turn around and she lights a cigarette for herself, one for me.

"That money was for Chad to start college with," she says. "Not for us to get fucking by on." It's one of the few times in over eighteen years that I've ever heard her complain about money. She's mad now, and she stops smoking and stares at the TV. "Just because you're trapped in a goddamned dead-end job doesn't mean he has to be." I look in the mirror again and I see her sitting next to me and I see the same thing she does. She turns back to me on the bed then.

"I'm sorry," she says. "It's just that I never expected it to be that bad. I thought they'd at least negotiate." It's no good telling her that nothing's final yet because she knows what the other plants have signed for, and that they've all had to take some kind of cut.

"I'll put in some applications with some other places this week." I'm talking to the TV again. "If anything comes through I might take it. It's going to be a drop in pay no matter what I do." She knows this won't happen, and I know it won't happen. Me getting another job that is.

"Why don't you let me ask him?" She's talking about her father, about asking him for money. It's the last thing in the world I want to do but tonight I think about it for a minute. She wanted to take the kids to Saskatchewan for Christmas this year, one last time before Chad leaves home, but now everything's up in the air again and she'll have to tell them we can't swing it. I put my arms around her then, and pull her down on top of me in the bed, wipe the sweat off her upper lip. I hold her close to me for a while and we let the fan blow some cold air over us, wait for the world to stop spinning. They wrap up the news and go on to the weather and I can smell her over the liniment and feel her nipples through her nightdress. She moves a little on top of me and I bury myself then. I bury myself so deep that my shoulder doesn't burn and I forget the smell of warm pig meat and the sound of the overhead rail, the eight hundred of us standing under there every day, waiting.

On Wednesday I take the afternoon off to go job-hunting and by the time I've been to six places I've got the routine down pretty good for someone who hasn't had to look for work in over eighteen years. I drop off the resumé Dianne did up for me or I fill out an application at the counter and someone checks it over before I go. This one's for a place on the loading docks at Manitoba Trucking, and I'm going through it with the HR guy.

"Do you have Grade Twelve, Paul?" They always know this but they always ask anyway and I always answer.

"No, but I was going to try for my GED at Red River College." I decide that after this one I'm going to lie about that part.

"Any other work experience? Tickets? Licences? Papers?" He's reading them off the application form in front of him. On mine the boxes are left empty, but I answer when he asks each question.

"Fork lift ticket?"

"No, but I can get it quick enough."

"And you've been at the plant how many years?" That's always on there too, along with my references. They never have much else to say to me, so I ask them when I'll hear from them and they always tell me the same thing.

"We're not hiring right now but we'll get back to you if anything comes up."

The hard part's not finding out they don't want me because I was in court or on the roads when I should have been in school, or knowing that I should have had the guts to do this years ago. All that's behind me now and I don't regret any of it just because I'm going to be up against a wall for a while. And it's not knowing that Dianne's going to have to put off going back to school because I can't even get a job pushing crates onto a tractor-trailer. Dianne's got stamina and she's got brains and she'll try again in a few years, and she'll make it too. The hard part's having to walk back into that plant with Chad every day, trying to hang on while I watch him count the days until he's out of there.

Chad usually finds his own rides to work and back because he's always got something on the go, but some mornings I get up early and drive him to the pool. I always stand behind the viewing window so I can see him there in the third lane. He's strong and even and he's so smooth you can barely see the water move around him when he swims. The pool is always quiet and while he does his laps I count them off, passing the time with him before I go to work.

On Friday morning we're heading down Regent with the windows open and so is everyone else. I'm tired today because I only slept about an hour before sunrise, after it finally cooled down. Chad's hair is still wet from swimming and he fills the front seat, his knees hooked up on the dash in front of him. I ask him how work is going.

"Okay, I guess," he says. "Pretty mindless work though." He's flipping through the stations on the radio and the DJ is going on about thundershowers later in the week. I don't answer him and he asks me if I'm going to take a package if they offer one. He doesn't find anything he likes so he keeps flipping through the stations.

"I can't see why you'd want to stay there if they'll pay you to leave," he says. "They're like a bunch of idiots most days."

He means the cartoon and the line stops and I'm thinking that I should have talked to him about it because I knew we'd be in negotiations this summer. But I really don't know what else to tell him, other than what we told him when he was eight years old. He doesn't seem to remember that so I don't bring it up. I just tell him that that's the way it is during negotiations and that it doesn't mean anything but you've still got to do it.

"Place'll be gone in a few years anyway," he says and the DJ goes into a big spiel about beer and burgers, another sunny day at the beach, hits of the sixties, seventies, eighties, and nineties. My shirt is soaked with sweat already and I feel like pulling off the road and sitting with him for a while but we're almost to Lagimodiere and there's no place to turn off so I keep driving. I fall in behind a load of pigs from Teulon and at the light I move into the lane alongside them. Their smell comes in through the car window and Chad's got the ball scores on now, so I clear my throat and swallow, try to talk over all the noise.

"I've been checking into a few places," I tell him. "If anything comes up, I think I'll look into it." The truck lets its air brakes out and starts gearing up so I don't hear most of what he says next. But I catch enough.

". . . dead . . . place like that . . . ten bucks an hour."

I don't look over at him. I just wait for what he said to settle into the car between us, hope that he doesn't say anything else. I can feel him watching me again, even if he doesn't realize it, because that's what I gave him when I promised him things would be different for him. The DJ is still going on about the heat wave and the weekend, and the truck is in front of us again so I drive into the plant behind it. By the time I stop I'm stuck to the vinyl and Chad hops out, stretches his knees. "I'll find my own way home today," he says and then he walks away from me. I watch him until he disappears into the door by the time clock and before I know it I've clocked in too and I'm feeling for the edge of the catwalk, staring at the wall in front of me and waiting for the first pig.

Even the line manager doesn't come out on the floor now. Only the foremen and the inspectors actually come out here, and only if they have to. Everyone else tries to stay clear until the talks are over. But today at about 1:15 the new guy in QA makes the mistake of coming out on the floor and the guys spot him at the boot dip next to the gutting table. They start banging their knives on the table and then it spreads down the line to the cutting floor and the coolers. There's a couple hundred people yelling "we'll get ours, you'll get yours" and all through the floor you can hear the sound of those knives, even with your ear defenders on. The guy is just out of college and he's never seen anything like this before so he backs his way out of there and heads for the office, doesn't even look back. There's two line stops before afternoon break and then after break it takes a half-hour before the line finally settles down again.

I can't see Chad from where I stand on the line but I hear about him in the parking lot after work. Jimmy's there, along with a couple of the younger guys from the cutting floor, and when I go to open my door Jimmy sticks his boot on my front bumper. "Looks like someone's going to have to have a chat with that son of yours, Paul," he says.

I pretend I don't know what he's getting at and ask, "Why's that, Jimmy?"

"Because while the rest of us were making ourselves heard in there today he stood around with his arms folded, not saying a goddamned word." I know what I'm supposed to say to that, but I just get into the front seat and start up. I put the car into gear and lean out the window with my foot on the brake.

"Fuck off, Jimmy," I say to him, and he takes his foot down then and moves away from the car. He's tired too, and he doesn't say anything else, but I can't just leave it there like that. "I'll see you Monday," I tell him and I drive away from the plant and head back down Lagimodiere and Regent in the evening traffic. When I come in through the backyard it smells like dry soil and bare wood and there's a note from Dianne saying she's shopping with the girls. I get a beer and sit out back until the breeze dies down at five o'clock, the time of the day on the prairies when it seems like nothing moves, not even a car on the street or the leaves on the trees. When I hear that I know I'm home.

We bought the house in East Kildonnan when I first went permanent after Chad was born. It's a storey and a half and it's the same size and shape as the other houses on the street, just a different colour and different shingles. It needs a new roof but other than that it's in good shape. Dianne's never complained that we couldn't afford something bigger but I know it took her a long time to call it home. She didn't mind the apartments too much because they were only temporary, but when we first moved in here she got homesick for a yard where you couldn't almost touch the back fence from the kitchen window. She made it hers after a while though, and once she did she never looked back. She hauled in soil for a garden and sand for the kids and then she planted flowers and grass. Later she built a little deck and a swing set, and even though there's only about twenty feet between the back step and the alley we spend all our weekends out there.

On Saturday the girls are trying on new school outfits while me and Dianne barbecue together. I'm flipping burgers and when I step back I see the girls already getting taller than Dianne, Chad's muscles bulking up like mine did when I first started at the plant. For a second I think about Jimmy in that parking lot, but it's only for a second. I learned a long time ago not to bring things like that home. Otherwise you never hang on.

Chad and Dianne start talking credits and courses and I try to follow them but after a while I start feeling the sun and the beer and the week at the plant and I get sleepy then. I'm listening to Chad, thinking that he knows what he's talking about and that I didn't do too bad with him when the burgers catch fire and Dianne sends me out of there. "Go on and have your beer, Paul," she says, and I don't argue with her. I stretch my shoulder and feel the heat on it and then I doze in the sun and the smoke for a while. When I wake up the girls are already eating and Dianne and Chad are still talking about colleges, and I've still got Sunday to go yet.

Sometimes I see things exactly like this. When things get so bad that I don't think I can hang on for another minute I close my eyes and I reach for something I know I can feel. I picture the four of them under the stars or in the barbecue smoke, and then I see Jimmy's face when I put my hand up for the yes vote, the new guy who bumped into his job after the buyout, Chad in the parking lot on his last day. I drive home along Lagimodiere or out to Dianne's farm with the windows down, find the edge of the deck under my bare toes, the moon in northern Saskatchewan. I remember Dianne's smell or the sound of her breathing and the minute passes, and I tell myself I don't mind.

About the Authors

Rosaria Campbell was born and raised in Campbell's Creek, Newfoundland, and has worked in agriculture since leaving there. In 1995 she completed an English degree at St. Mary's University, and in 2002 she won *The Fiddlehead*'s fiction prize. She has also studied at the Maritime Writers' Workshop and in the Mentor Program with the Writers' Federation of Nova Scotia. She lives in Wallace Station, Nova Scotia, where she is working on a collection of short stories. "Reaching" is her first piece of published fiction.

Hilary Dean is from Richmond Hill, Ontario, and now lives in Toronto. "The Lemon Stories" is an excerpt from "Lillypad Society," a novel currently in progress.

Dawn Rae Downton is an expatriate Newfoundlander who lives on Nova Scotia's South Shore. Her fiction has appeared in *The Fiddlehead*, the *Wascana Review*, *Descant*, *Pagitica*, *TickleAce*, and *Grain*. She also writes non-fiction, and her family memoir about Depression-era Newfoundland, *Seldom*, was judged one of the best books of 2002 by the editors of Amazon.ca. Her second memoir, *Diamond*, was published in 2003. She recently completed a novel set in occupied France during the Second World War, and is working on another, also with an historical French setting.

Anne Fleming was born in Toronto and lived in Kitchener-Waterloo for eight years before moving to Vancouver. Her first book, *Pool Hopping and Other Stories*, published by Polestar in 1998, was shortlisted for the Governor General's Award. Her novel, *Anomaly*, will be published by Raincoast Books in 2004.

"Gay Dwarves of America" was also nominated for a National Magazine Award.

Elyse Friedman's first novel, *Then Again*, was shortlisted for the 1999 Trillium Book Award. Her first book of poems, *Know Your Monkey*, will be published by ECW Press in fall 2003. Her new novel, *Morph*, is scheduled to be published by Crown in spring 2004. She lives in Toronto, and is currently working on a book of short stories.

Charlotte Gill was born in London, England, and raised in the United States and Canada. She now lives in Vancouver. She is a graduate of the M.F.A. program in Creative Writing at the University of British Columbia. Her work has appeared in *Event*, *The Fiddlehead*, *Grain*, *Zygote*, and *01:Best Canadian Stories*. Her non-fiction has been broadcast on CBC Radio. Her collection of stories, *Zanzibar*, is forthcoming from Thomas Allen in spring 2004.

Jessica Grant lives in St. John's, Newfoundland. She is currently working on a collection of short stories, to be published by The Porcupine's Quill in 2004. "My Husband's Jump" is her first published story.

Jacqueline Honnet was born in Scotland, and spent her early childhood in the Caribbean before moving to Canada. Her work has appeared in *filling Station*, *PRISM international*, *Event*, and *Room of One's Own*. She lives in Calgary, where she is currently at work on her first collection of short stories, *Limbo*.

S.K. Johannesen lives in Stratford, Ontario. He is the author of numerous short stories and essays. Pasdeloup Press has recently published his first novel, *Sister Patsy*, with illustrations by Virgil Burnett. He has completed the manuscript for a second novel and is working on a collection of short stories.

Avner Mandelman was born in Israel and served in the Israeli Air Force during the Six Day War. His stories were selected for *The Best American Short Stories* and the *Pushcart Prize*, and read over American Public Radio and in Symphony Space in New York City. *Talking to the Enemy*, a short-story collection, was published by Oberon Press in 1998 and won the Best Fiction Award from the Jewish Public Library of Montreal. A second collection, *Cuckoos*, will be published in fall 2003. He lives in Toronto with his two children and is working on a literary thriller.

Tim Mitchell has written two screenplays, one about fairies and the other about a girl king, and he is now writing a children's novel entitled *Plush*. One of his short stories won a National Magazine Award in 1999. He lives in Sooke, British Columbia.

Heather O'Neill lives in Montreal, where she is currently completing her first novel.

About the Contributing Journals

For more information about all the journals that submitted stories to this year's anthology, please consult *The Journey Prize Stories* Web site: www.mcclelland.com/jps

Broken Pencil is the magazine of zine culture and the independent arts. We review underground publications, including zines, indie-published books, videos, artworks, e-zines, and music. We run groundbreaking features on art, culture, and society from an independent perspective. We reprint from the best of the underground press. In each issue, the new fiction section of the magazine celebrates the edgy and the unpredictable. For a sample copy please send a $5 cheque or concealed cash to *Broken Pencil*. Editor: Emily Schultz. Submissions and correspondence: *Broken Pencil*, attention Fiction Editor, P.O. Box 203, Station P, Toronto, Ontario, M5S 2S7. Web site: www.brokenpencil.com

Descant is a quarterly journal, now in its third decade, publishing poetry, prose, fiction, interviews, travel pieces, letters, literary criticism, and visual art by new and established contemporary writers and artists from Canada and around the world. Editor: Karen Mulhallen. Managing Editor: Mary Newberry. Submissions and correspondence: *Descant*, P.O. Box 314, Station P, Toronto, Ontario, M5S 2S8. E-mail: descant@web.net Web site: www.descant.on.ca

Event, established in 1971, is published three times a year by Douglas College in New Westminster, B.C. It focuses on fiction, poetry, creative non-fiction, and reviews by new and established writers, and every spring it runs a creative non-fiction contest.

Event has won regional, national, and international awards for its writers. Editor: Cathy Stonehouse. Assistant Editor: Carolyn Robertson. Fiction Editor: Christine Dewar. Submissions and correspondence: *Event*, P.O. Box 2503, New Westminster, British Columbia, V3L 5B2. E-mail (queries only): event@douglas.bc.ca Web site: http://event.douglas.bc.ca

The Fiddlehead, Canada's longest-running literary journal, publishes poetry and short fiction as well as book reviews. It appears four times a year, sponsors a contest for poetry and fiction with two $1,000 prizes, including the Ralph Gustafson Poetry Prize, and welcomes all good writing in English, from anywhere, looking always for that element of freshness and surprise. Editor: Ross Leckie. Managing Editor: Sabine Campbell. Submissions and correspondence: *The Fiddlehead*, Campus House, 11 Garland Court, P.O. Box 4400, Fredericton, New Brunswick, E3B 5A3. E-mail (queries only): fiddlehd@unb.ca Web site: www.lib.unb.ca/Texts/Fiddlehead

filling Station magazine has been published on a non-profit basis by a volunteer editorial collective in Calgary for ten years, which strives to strike a balance among new, emerging, and established writers, and among local, national, and international writers. *filling Station* encourages submission of all forms of contemporary writing (poetry, fiction, one-act plays, essays, and book reviews). All submissions must be original and previously unpublished; simultaneous submissions are acceptable. Submission deadlines are March 15, July 15, and November 15 of each year. Managing Editor: Natalie Simpson. Submissions and correspondence: *filling Station*, Box 22135, Bankers Hall, Calgary, Alberta, T2P 4J5. E-mail: editor@fillingstation.ca

Grain magazine provides readers with fine, fresh writing by new and established writers of poetry and prose four times a year.

Published by the Saskatchewan Writers Guild, *Grain* has earned national and international recognition for its distinctive literary content. Editor: Elizabeth Philips. Editor as of fall 2003: Kent Bruyneel. Fiction Editor: Marlis Wesseler. Poetry Editor: Seàn Virgo. Submissions and correspondence: *Grain*, P.O. Box 67, Saskatoon, Saskatchewan, S7K 3K1. E-mail: grainmag@sasktel.net Web site: www.grainmagazine.ca

The Malahat Review is a quarterly journal of contemporary poetry and fiction by both new and celebrated writers. Summer issues feature the winners of *Malahat*'s Novella and Long Poem prizes, held in alternate years; all issues feature covers by noted Canadian visual artists and include reviews of Canadian books. Editor: Marlene Cookshaw. Assistant Editor: Lucy Bashford. Submissions and correspondence: *The Malahat Review*, University of Victoria, P.O. Box 1700, Station CSC, Victoria, British Columbia, V8W 2Y2. Web site: www.malahatreview.ca

The New Quarterly publishes fiction, poetry, interviews, and essays on writing. A two-time winner of the gold medal for fiction at the National Magazine Awards, with silver medals for fiction, poetry, and the essay, the magazine prides itself on its independent take on the Canadian literary scene. Recent achievements include "Wild Writers We Have Known," in which twenty-two writers who have worked extensively in the short-story form talk about what makes it work and how, and "Bad Men Who Love Jesus," which featured poems, stories, and theatre pieces, all bearing the same title, "Bad Men Who Love Jesus" – yes, really. Editor: Kim Jernigan. Submissions and cor-respondence: *The New Quarterly*, c/o St. Jerome's University, 200 University Avenue West, Waterloo, Ontario, N2L 3G3. E-mail: newquart@watarts.uwaterloo.ca Web site: http://newquarterly.uwaterloo.ca

Parchment was founded in 1992 by an editorial board of some of Canada's most distinguished writers, including Shel Krakofsky, Irving Layton, Seymour Mayne, Allan Gould, and others. As Canada's only Canadian Jewish journal of creative writing, *Parchment*'s mission is to provide an opportunity for new and established writers to express authentic Jewish-Canadian experiences and concerns – both historical and current – in the best poetry and short fiction being written in Canada. Because Jewish creative writing is usually regarded as too "ethnic" and/or "parochial" by mainstream Canadian literary journals, *Parchment* often provides the only opportunity for Canadian writers whose works reflect this experience to be published. *Parchment* accepts submissions of short fiction (up to 3,000 words in length), poetry, creative memoirs, and literary criticism. Editor: Adam Fuerstenberg. Submissions and correspondence: *Parchment*, Centre for Jewish Studies, Vanier 260, York University, 4700 Keele Street, Toronto, Ontario, M3J 1P3.

This Magazine is one of Canada's longest-publishing magazines of politics, culture, and the arts. Over the years, *This Magazine* has introduced the early work of some of Canada's most notable writers, poets, and critics, including Margaret Atwood, Naomi Klein, Dennis Lee, Lillian Allen, Tomson Highway, Evelyn Lau, Dionne Brand, Michael Ondaatje, Mark Kingwell, Lynn Crosbie, Lynn Coady, and Jason Sherman. *This Magazine* publishes new fiction in every issue, and poetry three times a year, as well as an annual literary supplement in the September/October issue. The magazine does not accept unsolicited submissions of fiction, poetry, or drama, but new writers are encouraged to enter the magazine's annual contest, The Great Canadian Literary Hunt. Editor: Julie Crysler. Submissions and correspondence: *This Magazine*, 401 Richmond St. W., #396, Toronto, Ontario, M5V 3A8. Web site: www.thismag.org

Submissions were also received from the following journals:

The Amethyst Review
(Truro, N.S.)

The Antigonish Review
(Antigonish, N.S.)

The Capilano Review
(North Vancouver, B.C.)

The Claremont Review
(Victoria, B.C.)

The Dalhousie Review
(Halifax, N.S.)

Exile
(Toronto, Ont.)

Green's Magazine
(Regina, Sask.)

lichen
(Whitby, Ont.)

The New Orphic Review
(Nelson, B.C.)

On Spec Magazine
(Edmonton, Alta.)

Pagitica in Toronto
(Toronto, Ont.)

Pottersfield Portfolio
(Sydney, N.S.)

Prairie Fire
(Winnipeg, Man.)

Prairie Journal
(Calgary, Alta.)

PRISM international
(Vancouver, B.C.)

Queen's Quarterly
(Kingston, Ont.)

Queen Street Quarterly
(Toronto, Ont.)

Room of One's Own
(Vancouver, B.C.)

Storyteller
(Ottawa, Ont.)

subTerrain Magazine
(Vancouver, B.C.)

Taddle Creek
(Toronto, Ont.)

The Journey Prize Stories
List of Previous Contributing Authors

* Winners of the $10,000 Journey Prize
** Co-winners of the $10,000 Journey Prize

I

1989

SELECTED WITH ALISTAIR MacLEOD

Ven Begamudré, "Word Games"
David Bergen, "Where You're From"
Lois Braun, "The Pumpkin-Eaters"
Constance Buchanan, "Man with Flying Genitals"
Ann Copeland, "Obedience"
Marion Douglas, "Flags"
Frances Itani, "An Evening in the Café"
Diane Keating, "The Crying Out"
Thomas King, "One Good Story, That One"
Holley Rubinsky, "Rapid Transits"*
Jean Rysstad, "Winter Baby"
Kevin Van Tighem, "Whoopers"
M.G. Vassanji, "In the Quiet of a Sunday Afternoon"
Bronwen Wallace, "Chicken 'N' Ribs"
Armin Wiebe, "Mouse Lake"
Budge Wilson, "Waiting"

2

1990

SELECTED WITH LEON ROOKE; GUY VANDERHAEGHE

André Alexis, "Despair: Five Stories of Ottawa"
Glen Allen, "The Hua Guofeng Memorial Warehouse"
Marusia Bociurkiw, "Mama, Donya"
Virgil Burnett, "Billfrith the Dreamer"
Margaret Dyment, "Sacred Trust"

Cynthia Flood, "My Father Took a Cake to France"*
Douglas Glover, "Story Carved in Stone"
Terry Griggs, "Man with the Axe"
Rick Hillis, "Limbo River"
Thomas King, "The Dog I Wish I Had, I Would Call It Helen"
K.D. Miller, "Sunrise Till Dark"
Jennifer Mitton, "Let Them Say"
Lawrence O'Toole, "Goin' to Town with Katie Ann"
Kenneth Radu, "A Change of Heart"
Jenifer Sutherland, "Table Talk"
Wayne Tefs, "Red Rock and After"

3
1991
SELECTED WITH JANE URQUHART

Donald Aker, "The Invitation"
Anton Baer, "Yukon"
Allan Barr, "A Visit from Lloyd"
David Bergen, "The Fall"
Rai Berzins, "Common Sense"
Diana Hartog, "Theories of Grief"
Diane Keating, "The Salem Letters"
Yann Martel, "The Facts Behind the Helsinki Roccamatios"*
Jennifer Mitton, "Polaroid"
Sheldon Oberman, "This Business with Elijah"
Lynn Podgurny, "Till Tomorrow, Maple Leaf Mills"
James Riseborough, "She Is Not His Mother"
Patricia Stone, "Living on the Lake"

4
1992
SELECTED WITH SANDRA BIRDSELL

David Bergen, "The Bottom of the Glass"
Maria A. Billion, "No Miracles Sweet Jesus"
Judith Cowan, "By the Big River"

Steven Heighton, "A Man Away from Home Has No Neighbours"
Steven Heighton, "How Beautiful upon the Mountains"
L. Rex Kay, "Travelling"
Rozena Maart, "No Rosa, No District Six"*
Guy Malet De Carteret, "Rainy Day"
Carmelita McGrath, "Silence"
Michael Mirolla, "A Theory of Discontinuous Existence"
Diane Juttner Perreault, "Bella's Story"
Eden Robinson, "Traplines"

5
1993
SELECTED WITH GUY VANDERHAEGHE

Caroline Adderson, "Oil and Dread"
David Bergen, "La Rue Prevette"
Marina Endicott, "With the Band"
Dayv James-French, "Cervine"
Michael Kenyon, "Durable Tumblers"
K.D. Miller, "A Litany in Time of Plague"
Robert Mullen, "Flotsam"
Gayla Reid, "Sister Doyle's Men"*
Oakland Ross, "Bang-bang"
Robert Sherrin, "Technical Battle for Trial Machine"
Carol Windley, "The Etruscans"

6
1994
SELECTED WITH DOUGLAS GLOVER;
JUDITH CHANT (CHAPTERS)

Anne Carson, "Water Margins: An Essay on Swimming by
    My Brother"
Richard Cumyn, "The Sound He Made"
Genni Gunn, "Versions"
Melissa Hardy, "Long Man the River"*
Robert Mullen, "Anomie"

Vivian Payne, "Free Falls"

Jim Reil, "Dry"

Robyn Sarah, "Accept My Story"

Joan Skogan, "Landfall"

Dorothy Speak, "Relatives in Florida"

Alison Wearing, "Notes from Under Water"

7

1995

SELECTED WITH M. G. VASSANJI;

RICHARD BACHMANN (A DIFFERENT DRUMMER BOOKS)

Michelle Alfano, "Opera"

Mary Borsky, "Maps of the Known World"

Gabriella Goliger, "Song of Ascent"

Elizabeth Hay, "Hand Games"

Shaena Lambert, "The Falling Woman"

Elise Levine, "Boy"

Roger Burford Mason, "The Rat-Catcher's Kiss"

Antanas Sileika, "Going Native"

Kathryn Woodward, "Of Marranos and Gilded Angels" *

8

1996

SELECTED WITH OLIVE SENIOR;

BEN MCNALLY (NICHOLAS HOARE LTD.)

Rick Bowers, "Dental Bytes"

David Elias, "How I Crossed Over"

Elyse Gasco, "Can You Wave Bye Bye, Baby?" *

Danuta Gleed, "Bones"

Elizabeth Hay, "The Friend"

Linda Holeman, "Turning the Worm"

Elaine Littman, "The Winner's Circle"

Murray Logan, "Steam"

Rick Maddocks, "Lessons from the Sputnik Diner"

K.D. Miller, "Egypt Land"

Gregor Robinson, "Monster Gaps"

Alma Subasic, "Dust"

9

1997

SELECTED WITH NINO RICCI;

NICHOLAS PASHLEY (UNIVERSITY OF TORONTO BOOKSTORE)

Brian Bartlett, "Thomas, Naked"

Dennis Bock, "Olympia"

Kristen den Hartog, "Wave"

Gabriella Goliger, "Maladies of the Inner Ear" * *

Terry Griggs, "Momma Had a Baby"

Mark Anthony Jarman, "Righteous Speedboat"

Judith Kalman, "Not for Me a Crown of Thorns"

Andrew Mullins, "The World of Science"

Sasenarine Persaud, "Canada Geese and Apple Chatney"

Anne Simpson, "Dreaming Snow" * *

Sarah Withrow, "Ollie"

Terence Young, "The Berlin Wall"

10

1998

SELECTED BY PETER BUITENHUIS; HOLLEY RUBINSKY;

CELIA DUTHIE (DUTHIE BOOKS LTD.)

John Brooke, "The Finer Points of Apples" *

Ian Colford, "The Reason for the Dream"

Libby Creelman, "Cruelty"

Michael Crummey, "Serendipity"

Stephen Guppy, "Downwind"

Jane Eaton Hamilton, "Graduation"

Elise Levine, "You Are You Because Your Little Dog Loves You"

Jean McNeil, "Bethlehem"

Liz Moore, "Eight-Day Clock"

Edward O'Connor, "The Beatrice of Victoria College"

Tim Rogers, "Scars and Other Presents"

Denise Ryan, "Marginals, Vivisections, and Dreams"

Madeleine Thien, "Simple Recipes"

Cheryl Tibbetts, "Flowers of Africville"

11

1999

SELECTED BY LESLEY CHOYCE; SHELDON CURRIE;

MARY-JO ANDERSON (FROG HOLLOW BOOKS)

Mike Barnes, "In Florida"

Libby Creelman, "Sunken Island"

Mike Finigan, "Passion Sunday"

Jane Eaton Hamilton, "Territory"

Mark Anthony Jarman, "Travels into Several Remote Nations of
    the World"

Barbara Lambert, "Where the Bodies Are Kept"

Linda Little, "The Still"

Larry Lynch, "The Sitter"

Sandra Sabatini, "The One With the News"

Sharon Steams, "Brothers"

Mary Walters, "Show Jumping"

Alissa York, "The Back of the Bear's Mouth" *

12

2000

SELECTED BY CATHERINE BUSH; HAL NIEDZVIECKI;

MARC GLASSMAN (PAGES BOOKS AND MAGAZINES)

Andrew Gray, "The Heart of the Land"

Lee Henderson, "Sheep Dub"

Jessica Johnson, "We Move Slowly"

John Lavery, "The Premier's New Pyjamas"

J.A. McCormack, "Hearsay"

Nancy Richler, "Your Mouth Is Lovely"

Andrew Smith, "Sightseeing"

Karen Solie, "Onion Calendar"